THE MARQUESS MEETS MISS NOBODY

ANNA AYSGARTH

To Saoirse

The Marquess Meets Miss Nobody
Copyright © 2018 by Anna Aysgarth

ISBN: 978-1-68046-677-5

Published by Satin Romance
An Imprint of Melange Books, LLC
White Bear Lake, MN 55110
www.satinromance.com

Published in the United States of America.

Cover Design by Ashley Redbird Designs

PROLOGUE

Yorkshire, 1799

$\mathscr{A}$s the girl looked from one to the other, she tried to make herself as tiny as possible because she knew she was the cause of their argument. Small and thin, her hair hung in greasy strands under a dirty grey cap, her woollen stockings were patched, and the pinafore she wore was grubby. She wiped her nose on her sleeve and hung her head. The Countess of Rockingham looked at her with a disgust she did not bother to conceal.

"I cannot believe you are serious about this, Rockingham." She felt no need to keep her voice down as it echoed through the marble hall. "Even if the child is indeed Jonathon's, your father disinherited him."

"Have a care, madam," the Earl of Rockingham replied. "If this child is Jonathon's, she is the daughter of an earl and should be addressed as 'lady.'"

"Are you not listening, William? Jonathon was disinherited. He was never Earl of Rockingham."

"Jonathon was the rightful earl. Father was wrong to disinherit him. If this child is his, the least I can do is to look after her, for my brother's sake." The earl's voice was quiet, but firm.

"Of course your father was right to disinherit Jonathon! He was set on a course of action which would damage the family's standing; nothing and no one could dissuade him." The countess's voice was shrill, and she paused to think for a moment before trying a different tactic. "Even if the child is Jonathon's, what proof is there that she is legitimate?"

"The woman who brought the child should be able to tell us." He reached for the bell cord. "She's some sort of warden at the Workhouse."

The countess turned to the girl. "What is your name, child?"

Deep blue eyes regarded her solemnly before she said, "'elen Rockin'am."

"How old are you, Helen?" The earl's voice was kinder than the woman's.

"Seven, sir."

The earl looked sharply at his wife. "It means nothing," she said frostily.

The warden was brought in, a thin woman with sharp features made even more severe by the drab uniform. The child shrank back as she entered the room, the earl noted. After bobbing a brief curtsey, she began. "'elen and 'er mother came to t'work'ouse six month ago. 'Er husband 'ad died an' she could not look after t'child what with another one on't way."

"Is there another child?" Rockingham asked quickly.

"Tis a sickly babe my lord, I doubt 'twill live the week," the woman said without a trace of emotion.

"And the mother?"

"Dead, sir, she died not long after t'birth. She were weak," she added defensively. "We did t'best we could."

"This is all very well," the countess put in, tapping her foot on the marble floor. "But I fail to see how any of this is a link between my husband and this child." She nodded toward the girl.

"Molly allus went on about 'ow she were married to gentry. To be 'onest, nobody believed 'er, but when she died, we found yon note." She nodded to the earl who looked at it once more.

Dear Sir,

We have never met, but I am the wife of your brother, Jonathon. It saddens me to tell you that Jonathon was killed when part of the mine collapsed. He had gone in to try to rescue some of the miners who had been trapped by an earlier roof fall. Since his death, my circumstances are reduced, and I can no longer care for my daughter Helen and the baby that Jonathon never lived to see.

I beg you, Sir, to take care of my children, I ask nothing for myself.

Yours sincerely,

Molly Rockingham

"The note is obviously a forgery. How could the daughter of a coal miner possibly pen that?" the countess said and sniffed.

"I believe, ma'am, Molly were t'daughter of t'mine manager. She were schooled, were Molly. There's summat else. She said, if nothin' else, this would convince yer." She looked at the child, "Give it to the gentleman." The child felt in her pocket and drew out a small package, tied with string.

"My God!" he exclaimed, drawing three silver teaspoons from the paper. "These are the missing spoons Mother gave to Jonathon when he left. They were specially crafted to her design," he said, eyeing his wife. "They were of a singular design and could never be forged."

"I do not understand," his wife said, frowning.

"When Father disinherited Jonathon, because, according to Father, he wanted to marry beneath him, it caused a rift between our parents. Father forbade Mother to help him in any way thinking, I suppose, that without money he would soon come crawling back. As he left, Mother gave Jonathon the teaspoons and told him that should he need help, he had only to return them," he explained. "There is now no doubt in my mind that this child is Jonathon's daughter."

"Nonsense, the child's mother could easily have stolen them," the countess's voice was harsh.

"Indeed so, but only the woman to whom they belonged would have known their significance. I repeat, my dear, I believe this child is Jonathon's legitimate daughter."

The Countess of Rockingham paused for a moment before turning to the warden. "Thank you for your part in this." She reached for the bell. "After some refreshment, we shall arrange for a cart to take you back to the poorhouse and I am sure my husband will be happy to give you a donation to keep up your invaluable work. We shall, of course, expect your complete discretion in this matter."

When the woman had gone, she turned to her husband. "I think the kindest thing we can do is to send the girl into the village to be apprenticed; perhaps to the seamstress so that she will have some means of supporting herself."

The earl looked at her in surprise. "What are you talking about? Helen will stay here."

His wife's eyes narrowed. "I suppose she could be trained as a lady's maid, Heaven knows a good maid is difficult to come by."

"Helen will not be trained as a lady's maid, or anything else. She will live here with us," he said firmly.

Her head snapped up. "You cannot possibly be serious. Look at her, she's filthy and I have no doubt that her hair is crawling, to say nothing of what diseases she may be infected with. She has no knowledge of society, no understanding of how to behave like a lady. It would be like bringing a feral cat into the house. Sending her away really would be the kindest thing."

The earl's eyes flared. "This child is the daughter of my older brother and as such she is in fact a lady. She will live with us and she will be brought up with our daughter as a lady. I am not to be swayed on this subject and there is to be no further discussion. Do you understand, Eunice?"

The countess nodded her head, but this was far from settled.

CHAPTER 1

London, 1812

The Westcott Ball was in full swing. A thousand candles burned in their sconces and were reflected in the great mirrors that decorated the ballroom. Swags of cream silk hung at the windows and the scent of lilies filled the room. Lady Westcott was particularly fond of lilies and every surface contained a vase of the elegant flowers. The cream and gold decor provided an excellent backdrop for the gowns of the women who moved like exotic birds in rich silks and brocades with diamonds, rubies, sapphires, and jewels of every hue sparkling at their throats, wrists, and ears.

Helen stood in an alcove, watching the cream of London society as they danced, gossiped, and flirted. Any excitement she felt at attending the ball had long gone. One glance as she arrived had confirmed her suspicions. Her aunt had gone out of her way to ensure that she looked as though she did not belong. Her gown was in precisely the shade of yellow that drained her complexion of life, and her chestnut curls had been tamed and drawn back into a tight chignon. At twenty, Helen had grown tall and slender, in contrast to her petite and dainty, fair-haired cousin, a fact that did not go unremarked in her aunt's waspish comments. Unlike the other women, Helen had no jewels to wear. She felt like a sparrow in the company of birds of paradise. Or rather, the poor relation, which she was.

Her cousin stood a little distance away, chatting to a group of her friends laughing at something she'd said. Helen had not been invited to join the young noblemen and ladies. Suddenly, Clarice turned and addressed her.

"Helen, I left my fan in the ladies' retiring room. Would you be so kind as to fetch it?"

"Of course, Lady Clarice." Helen replied, glad for a moment to escape the ballroom and knowing at the same time that Clarice had given a command phrased prettily as a request.

"Who is that?" she heard one of the gentlemen ask.

"Oh, nobody really, an orphan my parents took in as a child," Clarice replied smoothly.

"How kind of you to bring her to the ball."

"I like to think of her as a sister," Clarice simpered.

Helen did not hear the young man's reply. Instead of following the crush of women down the corridor, she slipped out onto the terrace. Suddenly, she needed air, before her temper got the better of her.

Helen learned long ago to swallow her anger and ignore the slights and insults she endured from Clarice with the collusion—if not encouragement—of her mother. Were it not for her uncle, she would have run away. He did treat her like his daughter, and perhaps that was the trouble. Ever since the Rockinghams had taken her in, Clarice had seen her as a threat, that instead of gaining a sister, she had gained a rival for her father's affections. It was the earl who had insisted Helen come to the ball, as he'd insisted she be included in all their social activities, but like many of the older gentlemen, he had retired to the card room as soon as he could. Her uncle never saw or heard the slights and taunts she was used to because when they were in his company her aunt and her cousin behaved impeccably. Helen did not speak of it, she merely determined that one day she would be free to live her own life without feeling as though she was an unwanted, inconvenient guest.

After the heat of the ballroom, the cool air of the terrace caused her to shiver. She leaned over the balustrade, inhaling the scent of the roses, and trying to calm down, determined not to give in to tears.

"If you are thinking of ending it all, I would suggest that throwing yourself off the terrace will be both messy and inefficient," an amused voice said, interrupting her thoughts.

Helen whirled round. The owner of the deep voice appeared to be standing in the shadows near the window. The light from the ballroom obscured her view, throwing him into silhouette, but from what she could tell, the stranger was tall and broad-shouldered. She could just make out the glittering diamond pin on his white neckcloth.

"I beg your pardon, sir, I did not know you were there," she stammered, knowing that, were she, a single young woman, found alone on the terrace with a man, it would be her ruination.

"Evidently," he agreed. "But as I happened upon you and persuaded you not to end it all, I think we might become introduced. I as your hero and you as a tragic heroine."

"Hero? Tragic heroine? Nonsense," she retorted.

He chuckled. "I am devastated. I come upon a young woman and offer to be her champion, her knight in shining armour, and what does she do? She snorts in derision."

Helen rolled her eyes. "I thank you, sir, but I was not about to end it all, so your services as champion, knight, or anything else are not required, and," she added, "I most definitely did not snort."

"Then why are you here? I could swear that when you came out, I distinctly heard a sniffle." His voice was softer, closer.

"I merely came out to take some air and relief from the heat of the ballroom, and now I must go. I have to fetch something, and I shall be missed." Helen turned, her breath caught in her throat. He was standing close enough for her to catch the scent of sandalwood and although his features were still obscured, she could make out a strong jaw and straight nose.

Without warning, Helen felt his hands on her arms, and shocked that he had touched her, she took a step backward and felt the cold stone of the balustrade. Even more shocking was that he had removed his gloves, and his hands were warm against her cool skin. Yet she felt hot at the same time. A tremor shot through her body.

"You are cold, you had best return," he said quietly. "No doubt a fond mama or sweetheart will be looking for you."

Helen laughed. "Oh, I assure you, sir, I shall be missed." Most likely by Lady Clarice for want of her fan, but that much she digressed.

"I believe we have yet to be introduced, Miss...?"

"Nobody, sir, I am nobody, and now I must go."

Before she had a chance to move, his thumb gently traced the outline of her lips causing her to gasp in shock. This was more than enough to ruin her, though, if she were being honest, it felt thrilling. Instead, she demanded, "What are you doing? You are being much too forward, risking the damage of my reputation beyond repair if anyone should see." She wriggled out of his grasp and disappeared into the shadows at the end of the terrace.

Lord James Tremaine, Marquess of Woodville, watched her leave, but made no attempt to follow. Her lips had felt so soft beneath his fingers, he wanted to know how they would feel beneath his own. He was intrigued. He would, he decided, find out who "Miss Nobody" was by the end of the ball.

CHAPTER 2

"**You** ou took your time," Lady Clarice snapped.

"There was a crush, but here it is." Helen held out the fan.

"You will never guess who has arrived," Lady Eunice said as she joined her daughter. "Lord James Tremaine, the Marquess of Woodville, adopted heir to his elderly relative the Duke of Bainbridge. His brother is the Duke of Whitney. Imagine, two brothers to be dukes outside of the royal family! They are one of the most well-connected and powerful families in the country."

Helen could not help but smile at Lady Eunice's transparency; the higher the title, the better. Any thought of knights, baronets, or even titled lords as potential husbands for Clarice was forgotten. A man who would one day bear the title of Duke was the ultimate prize. "And," she went on, "I can ensure that you are introduced. I was at school with his mother. That will give you a great advantage," she said complacently.

"Now, Clarice, go and attend to your appearance. Helen, you will go and help. When you return, I shall introduce you. Helen, you will remain available to be of assistance should you be required, but there is to be no forward behaviour. On no account should you address his lordship."

"Of course, your ladyship." Helen did not expect to be introduced, nor did she desire it. Her observations as she grew up in the shadow of her cousin led her to the conclusion that females only seemed to be of worth as chattels. They had to obey their fathers then their husbands, denied any form of expression other than that dictated by virtue of their sex. Many times, she had seen Clarice's friends paint beautiful pictures which would never be recognized as works of art. Her own work as a writer would never be published. If anything, females of rank would only be recognized, if they were recognized at all, as dutiful daughters, obedient wives, and good mothers.

"Of course, Lord Tremaine was only a second son and was not in line to inherit anything," Clarice explained as they walked toward the ballroom. "The Duke of Bainbridge is a distant elderly relative of his mother and has adopted Tremaine as his heir. It is quite something for two brothers to be dukes outside of the royal family." Clarice turned to Helen. "Now, if you are introduced, be sure to do nothing to disgrace yourself or the family. Remember what Mama said: he is a member of one of the most powerful and influential families in the country, he needs a wife, and I intend that it should be me."

When they returned, they found Lady Eunice talking to a handsome older woman who was introduced as Lady Tremaine. A tall man stood close by, disinterestedly watching the figures on the dance floor. He was probably the tallest man in the room and certainly towered over the two women. His dark evening clothes fitted him to perfection emphasizing the width of his shoulders and the length of his muscular legs. As he turned, Helen stifled a gasp as she noticed the diamond pin on the white neckcloth. She had already met him, though she had not realized how handsome he was: his dark hair, strong jaw, and straight nose were eclipsed by startling grey eyes fringed with black lashes, eyes that felt as though they could see into her soul.

"It has been such a long time, please come and call." Lady Eunice was smiling her social smile. "Ah, here is my daughter, Clarice."

The man bent over Clarice's hand. "A pleasure to meet you." When he stood up, he looked toward Helen. There was a pause before he said, "And this is?"

Lady Eunice turned to Helen as though the marquess had not spoken. "Go fetch some lemonade, dear? Lady Tremaine and I are parched."

Helen needed no second bidding. At the door, she turned, feeling that she was being watched and her eyes were caught in the speculative gaze of Lord Tremaine.

Helen carefully carried the glasses of lemonade back to the two women who were sitting and chatting on the gilt chairs at the edge of the ballroom. A quick glance at the dancers showed her that Lord Tremaine was dancing a quadrille with Clarice. She could not help noticing that he moved with grace.

"Thank you, dear." Lady Eunice took the glasses and handed one to her friend. "Now why don't you run along and—"

"I do not believe we were introduced, my dear," Lady Tremaine interrupted.

"This is Rockingham's niece," Lady Eunice said through gritted teeth.

Lady Tremaine's eyebrows shot up. "Jonathon's daughter? I had no idea."

"Jonathon died. Helen has been with us since she was seven or eight."

Lady Tremaine's eyes narrowed. "I remember now, did he not want to marry someone his father considered entirely unsuitable?"

"A miner's daughter." Lady Eunice could barely contain the revulsion in her voice.

"I beg your pardon, ma'am, but my mother was the daughter of the mine manager, an engineer, and a well-educated and kind woman." Helen's voice was low but firm.

"Whatever she was, old Rockingham threatened to disinherit him if he went ahead with the wedding. When both her parents died, she came to us and we have brought her up as one of the family," Lady Eunice continued as though Helen had not spoken.

"It was quite a scandal at the time, I believe," Lady Tremaine mused. "Yet, with my eldest son's wife, I learned not to judge a book by its cover." She smiled at Helen.

The quadrille ended, and James escorted Clarice back to her mother before turning to Helen, "Would you grant me the honour of the next dance?"

Helen shook her head. "I do not dance, my lord." She could not deny that his manners were perfect, and having danced with Clarice, he felt obliged to ask her.

"Of course, you must dance." Lady Tremaine's eyes sparkled with mischief. Lady Eunice smiled as though in encouragement, but it did not reach her eyes.

James needed no further encouragement. He had not been able to get this woman out of his mind since their encounter on the terrace. He could not help grinning as the quartet struck up a waltz. He could feel the tension in her body as he took her in his arms.

Helen kept her head down, fixing her gaze on the diamond on his neckcloth.

James looked down at her, and although her chestnut hair was drawn into a tight chignon, a style intended to make her look like a schoolmistress, it could not disguise her fine skin and delicate features. He wondered why she seemed determined to appear plain and dowdy. Miss Nobody was a mystery, and James had always loved a mystery. He recognized her as the woman from the terrace, the minute he had turned around, although he had been in the shadows, the light from the windows had illuminated her clearly. Now, for some reason, he wanted to see the colour of her eyes.

"I believe it is customary for dance partners to look at each other and exchange the occasional word," he drawled.

"I cannot converse, my lord. I am trying to concentrate." Her alto voice was slightly husky. His eyes widened slightly: a woman's voice had never aroused him before.

"Then let me make it easier for you." He drew her closer, scandalously close.

Helen could feel her whole body respond as her breasts touched the smooth material of his evening jacket. She almost gasped as his muscled thigh brushed hers. Her head shot up. "What are you doing? People are looking, they will think—"

"People will think what they will; neither I nor you can control what others think. I am merely holding you like this so you may follow my lead, relax, and enjoy the dance. Or at least try to look as though you are." Her eyes were the deepest blue he had ever seen, almost the colour of cornflowers. He was fascinated.

"Relax? How am I supposed to relax when every eligible woman is looking at you as though you are some kind of Adonis and I am some kind of evil siren come to lure you to your death?" she muttered.

He grinned. "You think I am some kind of Greek god? I am flattered."

"I did not say that," she responded firmly.

"I am crushed," he said, sounding anything but.

"Oh, come, my lord. You cannot be unaware of the prize you are considered to be. Apparently, every unmarried female here fancies you should choose her as your future duchess, to say nothing of their mothers' ambitions."

"Apparently," he agreed, wondering idly whether the shade of her beautiful eyes might change with her emotions and wanting to find out. Wanting very much to find out.

He silenced further conversation by performing a series of turns, enjoying the feel of Helen in his arms. He could not explain his sudden attraction to her, she was not the cool blonde he usually favoured, a thought that caused his smile to slip momentarily. She seemed determined to appear plain with her hair scraped back and the frankly hideous gown. Yet there was something about her, definitely something that intrigued and excited him.

"Do I take it that you are not among the young ladies who wish to snare themselves a duke, or at least the heir to one?" he asked, slowing the pace again.

Helen laughed. "My future does not lie in that direction, my lord."

He quirked an eyebrow and waited for further explanation.

"I am sure your lordship would not want to sully his noble lineage with one such as me," she said calmly. The music stopped, and they walked back to the two older women who were now surrounded by Clarice and her friends. Word had quickly spread of Lord James Tremaine's presence and each girl was hoping for an introduction. James noticed Helen's smile as they approached. "You find something amusing?"

She turned, and the smile broadened. "I believe the ballroom is like the jungle, my lord, and you would do well to remember in the jungle, although the lion is the king of beasts, the lionesses do the hunting." He could hear the amusement in her voice as she quickly curtseyed and disappeared in the throng.

CHAPTER 3

*J*ames was already eating a hearty helping of eggs and bacon when his brother entered the breakfast room. "I did not expect to see you this early, brother," Robert Tremaine, Duke of Whitney, said as he helped himself to coffee, a blend he had imported especially from the Indies. "Though I thoroughly understand why you would need to go to White's after the ball. Why is it none of the celebrated hostesses think of serving some decent liquor at these functions?" he grumbled good-naturedly.

"I believe they think the young men behave badly enough as it is."

"They may have a point," he conceded. "I was surprised that you went to the ball in the first place. I have not known you to attend a ball since—"

"Arabella jilted me?" James finished for him.

It was true. Five years ago, Arabella Walmesly had famously jilted him days before the wedding. Having survived the scandal of stealing the Whitney diamonds in a moment of madness, she had spent time raising money to build a school. She had not sought to be recognized for her work, but recognition had come, she had become famous, and she had enjoyed every moment of it. James had supported her, stood by her, loved her, and introduced her to the man she would betray him for.

James had met Peter Hoyland at the Military Academy in Woolwich. Arabella met him at their engagement celebration. A week before the wedding, he received a message from Arabella. She had fallen in love with Hoyland and they were going to make a new life in America. She apologized, but Hoyland was rich and would ensure that her father could retain his place in society, his debts would be settled, and the shame of bankruptcy would be avoided. As a second son with few prospects of inheritance, James knew he could not offer Arabella the life she craved. Her school was running with the excellent head teacher she had appointed, and she was no longer needed except by Hoyland. They never made it; their boat sank off the coast of Newfoundland.

On the surface, James had recovered from the loss of his fiancée, but underneath, he had suffered, his easygoing attitude to life had gone, he had become harder—necessarily—to survive. He had sought and received a posting abroad and stayed away from London and society if possible. As well as working for the government, he had invested wisely and had become a man of great wealth, with interests in shipping, banking, and commerce.

It was his success that brought him to the attention of the elderly Duke of Bainbridge, his mother's second cousin. The old man had no sons, and as a favourite of the old king, had been granted permission to name his heir. He had met with James and offered him the duchy. All James had to do was reside primarily in Britain, marry, and produce an heir. James had accepted, though in truth the title meant little to him, but he genuinely liked the old man and knew how much it would please his mother. More importantly, at one-and-thirty he was growing tired of his rootless life. He wanted what his brother had with Emily and what he thought he might have had with Arabella: a wife, and in time, children.

"I needed to go to White's to clear my head," James replied.

"Of course you did. Sinking almost a bottle of brandy is well known for clearing the senses," his brother agreed with a grin. "The betting book is already half full with wagers as to which young lady will be fortunate to wed you by Christmas."

"In that case, the quality of White's has definitely gone down," James grumbled.

"Oh, come, brother, any man with a title, especially a man who will one day become a duke, has the bones of his private life picked over daily. The ton is like a flock of vultures and the women are the worst." Robert laughed at James' disgusted look.

"So who is the favourite?" James smeared a generous helping of marmalade onto his toast.

"Curiosity got the better of you?" Robert smirked.

"Curiosity about what?"

Neither man had heard Emily, Duchess of Whitney, enter the room. Both men stood as she came around the table to greet them. "James, it is lovely to see you again. I am so sorry we could not go to the ball with you last night, but the reception for the Austrians was something we were unable to ignore. Still," she added, her eyes sparkling with curiosity, "I believe you had a most interesting evening."

"I assume there is a full account of my movements in this morning's *Times*?" he responded drily.

"Oh, *The Times* has nothing like the speed of the servants' grapevine, and they are positively snail-like when compared to my mother-in-law." She poured herself tea and nibbled a piece of toast before adding, "So, do tell, is it to be Lady Clarice Rockingham?"

James' head shot up. "Lady Clarice?" he spluttered. "What on earth gave you that idea?"

"When two mamas have their heads together at a ball, and one is the mother of the heir to a dukedom and the other is the mother of an eligible young lady on the marriage mart, tongues begin to wag, and people begin to put two and two together," Emily explained patiently. "And you did dance with her, twice."

James smiled. "My dear sister-in-law, should ladies ever be persuaded to turn their talents for gleaning information to military matters, we should know our enemies' secrets before they know them themselves."

"One likes to be well-informed." Emily grinned back at him. "Now stop procrastinating and tell us all."

"As it happens, there was a young woman who caught my attention."

"I knew it," Emily said and grinned at her husband. "That is five guineas you owe me."

"What, even my own family is betting on my marital prospects? I suppose I should at least be thankful you are not in the betting book at White's," James grumbled.

"No point in getting huffy about it, brother. You have not been out of the country so long that you have forgotten how society works. I should not be surprised if a line were not forming, as we speak, of hopeful young women and their mamas."

"Lady Clarice is an acknowledged beauty," Emily put in. "She is also considered to be a highly accomplished young lady."

"Sounds like perfect duchess material to me," Robert agreed.

"I was merely being polite regarding Lady Clarice," James responded.

"Then which young lady is responsible for that look on your face?" As ever, his sister-in-law was not one to beat about the bush.

James smiled as he thought of the woman who had attracted his attention, the woman he could not get out of his mind. "There was someone," he said thoughtfully.

There was a pause before Emily burst out, "Who?"

James shook his head. "That is the trouble, I do not know."

"Were you not introduced to her?"

"That is the thing, I was partly introduced."

"Forgive me for stating the obvious, brother, but one is either introduced or one is not, there really is no middle ground," Robert said, taking a bite of toast.

James considered a moment, deciding that now was not the time to disclose his encounter with the mysterious young woman on the terrace. "I was introduced to Lady Clarice and this other young woman was there. I think she was part of their party, but she was not introduced and was sent off on an errand before I could catch her name." *Like a servant*, he thought suddenly. "I did, however, dance with her." Emily probably already knew from her various sources. "Encouraged, I might add, by Mother."

Emily's eyes widened. "Then your mother must know who this mystery young lady is. Your mother would never countenance an unsuitable match."

Robert laughed at his wife and leaned over to stroke her arm. "She countenanced you," he teased.

"I might remind you, Your Grace, that your mother is of the same opinion as I, that you are lucky to have me," she shot back, her eyes dancing with mischief.

James groaned. "Oh, really, it's much too early in the morning to witness one of your disgusting displays of marital harmony. Besides, I need you to help me find Miss Nobody."

CHAPTER 4

"Helen, Mother says you must come at once." Clarice was breathless as she entered Helen's room, as usual, without waiting for an invitation. "The Marquess of Woodville and his mother are here." Helen put down her pen and looked up. "I cannot imagine he has come to visit me," she said, sliding the sheets of paper into a neat pile.

"Of course not," Clarice scoffed, "but Mother intends to take Lady Tremaine on a tour of the gardens and you are to act as chaperone while I speak with Tremaine. Just think," she added, her eyes narrowing in speculation, "in a few months, I will be a marchioness, and by all accounts, a duchess in a year."

Helen looked at her cousin with a degree of pity, although in Clarice's mind everything was arranged. She would probably want to go to the modiste tomorrow to order her wedding trousseau, but Helen's observations at social occasions had taught her otherwise. Tremaine was the most eligible bachelor of the season, that was certainly true, and Lady Eunice and Lady Tremaine were friends, which always helped, but Clarice was only one of many. There were mamas who would lay their daughters out like carpet if they thought Lord James Tremaine might choose them, such was the competition for the eventual title of Your Grace.

"You need to tidy your hair and wash the ink from your fingers,

Helen. I do not want Tremaine to think we are uncivilized," Clarice said, already half-closing the door. "Five minutes," she added over her shoulder.

The last person on earth Helen wanted to be in a room with was Lord James Tremaine, as even the thought of it made her heart race. She had not been able to forget how it felt to be held in his arms, so close that she felt the strength and heat of his body. She did not want to sit and watch Clarice flirt with him. She picked up a book; she had always been able to lose herself in reading. If she had to be in the same room, she was determined that she would use the time profitably. She ignored Clarice's instructions regarding her hair. Lord Tremaine would probably not notice how she looked, and if he did, he would not care.

Lady Tremaine and her aunt were sitting in pale-blue silk-covered chairs by the fireplace, and Lord Tremaine was standing by the walnut side table near the window with Clarice who was showing him her watercolours. It was a sign of how important this visit was considered by Lady Eunice that it was taking place in the formal blue drawing room rather than the smaller morning room. This room had been designed by Helen's grandfather to impose and impress: the combination of rich dark-blue drapes and pale silk wallpaper contrasted with the gilt chandeliers and mirrors. A grand pianoforte stood at one end of the room and sofas and chairs in various shades of blue were scattered throughout, yet still the room seemed large, and to Helen, cold and impersonal. Full-length portraits of her grandparents were on either side of the white marble fireplace; her grandfather whom she had never met looked as stern and unbending in paint as he had been in life. Her grandmother, whom she loved dearly, had clearly been a great beauty.

"Ah, Helen," her aunt said rising. "I am about to take Lady Tremaine for a tour of the hothouses and gardens; perhaps you would be so good as to remain with your cousin."

"Of course, Aunt. Lady Tremaine." She curtseyed and went to sit on a sofa and opened her book. Within minutes, she was absorbed and unconsciously kicked off her slippers and tucked her feet on the sofa. She was startled to hear Clarice's voice in her ear. "Really, Helen, you are too bad. His lordship did you the courtesy of asking what you were reading."

Helen looked up, struggling to bring her brain from what was on the page to the two people who were now standing in front of her, Clarice frowning, Lord Tremaine grinning broadly.

"Oh, it's the work of a female writer," she said while rapidly trying to retrieve her slipper which had somehow gotten under the sofa.

"Allow me." James could hardly keep the amusement from his voice as he bent and picked up the slipper. Helen gasped as he took her foot in his hand and slid the slipper back on. "There you are, Cinderella, you shall go to the ball."

"Thank you, sir," she stammered. "That was very—"

"Charming?" he interrupted. "As in the prince?"

"Forward," she shot back. "As in how reputations are ruined."

He put his hand on his heart in mock regret. "I apologize for any offense," he said, though in truth he did not regret his impulsive action at all. How was it this little strip of a thing could arouse him without having a clue as to the effect she was having? When he held her foot, it was as though a bolt of lightning had shot through his entire being. She had narrow feet and shapely legs, that much he had seen, now he wanted to see more.

"You were telling his lordship what you are reading," Clarice cut in. "Helen always has her nose in a book, or if not, she sits scribbling away," she explained.

"How interesting."

Helen felt herself blush under the curious gaze of the unpredictable man in front of her. His eyes were grey, almost like molten silver, fringed with thick, dark lashes, and she almost felt hypnotized when she looked at him. She licked her lips nervously and lowered her eyes. James almost groaned at the sight of her tongue, clearing his throat loudly instead. "Tell me about the book that has you so absorbed, Lady Helen."

Helen's head snapped up. "I have no title, sir." Where had he been given that impression?

"Helen is just Helen," Lady Clarice put in quickly. "Now, I believe you were about to tell his lordship about the book you are reading."

Helen hesitated. Once Lady Eunice knew about the book she had no doubt it would be removed, however, there was nothing she could do to avoid the subject. "It is *The Rights of Woman* by Mrs. Mary Wollstonecraft."

James' eyebrows shot up. "How very modern, not to say radical. I must say I am surprised, given Wollstonecraft's somewhat tarnished reputation, that she is approved reading in this household," he drawled.

"That, sir, is exactly the sort of attitude that Mrs. Wollstonecraft challenges."

James was not only intrigued, he was enjoying seeing the colour in Helen's cheeks and the flash of passion darken her eyes. It reminded him of their brief encounter at the ball. He began to wonder if her eyes would darken when he kissed her, which he fully intended to do, and soon. "And what does Mrs. Wollstonecraft advocate?" he asked smoothly.

"The basic premise is that women are not inferior to men, it is just that they are lacking in education. Were they to have access to the same standards of education as men, they would be able to play a larger part in life," Helen said, determined to keep her voice firm.

"Oh, come, Helen. Women will never be able to play a part in public life. We are the weaker sex and our part in life is to be good, obedient wives and mothers. That is the contribution we make to life, is that not so, my Lord?" Clarice smiled.

"Lady Clarice has a point," James agreed. "Women are the weaker sex. It is the duty of gentlemen to protect them, and," he added, "all the great art, scientific discoveries, and inventions have been made by men."

"That is exactly my point," Helen burst out. "I concede that women are physically the weaker sex, and you are right, men have made the great advancements, but only because women are not educated in these matters. Whilst you are encouraged in matters of science and mathematics, we have to be content with embroidery and flower-arranging." She wrinkled her nose.

James could not help but laugh at her disgusted tone, though what she said gave him pause for thought. He had never much considered the life of a woman before. Most of the women he knew did indeed do a lot of sewing to no apparent purpose, and they filled their days with…well, he did not truly know what. It occurred to him that he would not be content with a life without purpose and challenge, and neither it seemed would Helen Rockingham.

"Really, Helen, I am sure his lordship has heard enough of this nonsense," Clarice snapped. "I must apologize if my cousin has offended you, my lord. I am sure you will want a decorative and accomplished wife to support you in your public life."

"No man would deny it." James laughed. "But now, ladies, the weather is fine, would you care to accompany me for a drive in the park?"

Clarice's eyes lit up. "I am sure we may, we have no other

engagement. I shall tell Mama. Helen, fetch our bonnets and shawls," she commanded.

---

*T*he day was fine and warm and within moments, Helen was seated opposite Clarice. They had frequent stops as they encountered other gentlemen and ladies who were taking advantage of the fair weather. Lord James Tremaine was known to many and greetings after his long absence had to be exchanged. She knew her role and kept her head turned to the side as a good chaperone should, but he was determined to introduce her to everyone they met. Before long, they were joined by the Earl of Redcar who had been at school and Oxford with Lord James, he rode alongside for a short while before suggesting that they take a turn round the lake.

As Clarice descended from the carriage, Redcar tucked her hand in the crook of his arm saying, "Lady Clarice, you were saying how fond of flowers you are…perhaps we should walk this way, I believe there is a particularly fine display of agapanthus. Perhaps you might consider them for a watercolour…" his voice became faint as they disappeared down the path.

James could not help but smile. Redcar had taken the slightest nod of his head as the hint he had intended it should be and left him alone with Helen. They were still in earshot and in theory each girl was chaperone to the other. "Shall we, Miss Rockingham?" He offered his arm. Helen took it as lightly as she could, and her eyes widened in surprise when he pulled it tightly and placed his own hand firmly on top of hers. Through the material of his jacket, there was no mistaking the hardness of his muscles.

James looked down at her. "So, Miss Rockingham, what shall we talk about? The scandalous cost of bonnet ribbons perhaps? Or the latest fashion in hairdressing? I myself am appalled at the cost of ball gowns."

Helen rolled her eyes. "I have no idea of the cost of bonnet ribbons. If I have to trim a bonnet, I merely look for some Clarice has discarded. I imagine I am as much interested in such things as you are, my lord. Unless you have a secret penchant you wish to share," she added impishly. James paused before he replied seriously, "I must confess, madam, I leave the trimming of my bonnets to my valet."

He smiled at Helen's laugh, and the low, husky chuckle instantly made his body harden. "So if we are not to talk about fashion, tell me something of yourself. How did you come to be the Earl of Rockingham's ward?"

He could feel Helen tense and her face became guarded. "It is not something I may speak of, sir."

"May not?"

"There was a scandal and my uncle, the earl, has been good to me. I should not want to rake up old stories which may embarrass him."

James stopped and put his hands on her shoulders, bringing her round to face him. "Miss Rockingham, I should very much like you to consider me a friend. I assure you there is nothing in your past that will colour my opinion of you. Unlike some of our less-enlightened acquaintances, I do not believe you are either responsible or to be blamed for mistakes that were made before you were born. If indeed a man and a woman falling in love can be considered a mistake," he spoke quietly.

As he watched the emotions play across her face, all he wanted to do was to take her in his arms and protect her. She was a young, vulnerable woman who had experienced the harshness of life and it made him angry that she was judged by a hypocritical society as unfit to be one of them.

Helen took a breath. "Very well, I will tell you what I remember, which is not much, and of what I have been told, then perhaps you will understand why it is best that I remain nobody to you."

They walked down the path for a moment while Helen gathered her thoughts. In truth, she did not really want James to know the sordid story of her past because she knew that once he was aware of her origin, he would most likely want nothing more to do with her, which was for his best interest if not hers. She took a steadying breath.

"My mother was the daughter of a mine manager and engineer who was in charge of one of the mines owned by the late Earl of Rockingham."

"Your grandfather?"

Helen nodded. "My father was his eldest son. He was interested in engineering and started visiting the mine to learn more about how mining was done and particularly how safety could be improved, as there were many accidents and injuries and he wanted to change things. He began spending time at the manager's cottage and fell in love with his daughter, my mother. When my grandfather learned of the affair, he threatened to disinherit my father. It did not matter that my mother was both educated and cultured, she was not of the right class. My father refused to give up my mother, they married, and I was born. My grandfather made good on his promise."

"I have not heard anything yet that is so awful," James said softly, willing Helen to know that the circumstances of her birth meant nothing to him.

"Ah, we have not come to that part yet, sir. As you surmise, my early childhood was not an unhappy one. We lived in a small cottage next to my grandparents." She smiled at the memory. "My grandpapa would fashion toys for me, dolls and animals carved from wood, grandmother played the pianoforte and taught me songs, my mother taught me to read and write. I have few memories of my father. One was him returning from a trip to buy equipment for the mine, and he brought me some paints and brushes."

"And the other," James prompted.

Helen laughed. "It is not so fond. I had wandered off, no one knew where I was, my parents were frantic. When I returned, my father spanked me, and I was not allowed to leave the house for a week."

"And did this cure you of your roaming tendencies?"

"It most certainly did," she said and frowned. "A few days later, there was the accident and I never saw my father again. There was an explosion, part of the mine collapsed. The cries of the trapped miners could be heard so it was decided to try and rescue them, and my father led the rescuers. They did not get far before another part of the mine collapsed; only the last two men at the back escaped and told of what happened."

Again, Helen paused. It had been a long time since she had allowed herself to remember the story. "After the accident, my mother, grandmother, and I had to leave our homes because they belonged to the mine. We had nowhere else. We went to the Workhouse and my grandmother died soon after."

James could feel her shudder. "But what of your grandpapa?"

"He was in the mine at the time of the explosion."

"And your other grandfather? He did nothing to help?" He was incredulous. "He would rather see his own grandchild, his own flesh and blood, in the Workhouse rather than lift a finger to help?"

"I can only think that he blamed my mother, for she caused him to lose his son twice," she said simply.

"If this is too distressing for you, you need not go on."

She shook her head. "No, after years of silence, I find I want to tell you. I want someone to know the truth."

James nodded. "I am privileged that you do me the honour of telling me." He was, in truth, astounded by her story. It was worse than he could have imagined. The woman before him was more of a lady than those born to a life of rich idleness could ever be. If ever a woman was deserving of the title Lady, here she was, and he was going to make damn sure she got it.

"I did not know, but my mother was with child when we went to the Workhouse. She did not long survive the birth, nor did the babe." Her huge eyes filled with tears. "I never thought of it before, but I do not know if I had a brother or sister."

This time James did not hesitate. He pulled her to him, stroking her back as she sobbed, trying to soothe the hurt she had buried for so long. Eventually, her sobs subsided, and she stepped back. "I apologize, Lord Woodville."

"Please stop. What you have told me would make the devil himself weep. But how did you come to find your rightful family?"

"Apparently, the last time my father saw the old earl, there was a terrible scene and my father was thrown out. My grandmama grabbed his hand, placing something within it, and told him that should he ever need help he should send them and she would find a way to help. As she lay dying, my mother begged the warden to send me to my father's family. All I have left of either of them is the note she wrote."

"What was it your grandmama gave him? Do you not still have that?"

"They were three silver teaspoons from a particular set. When I returned with them, Lady Rockingham insisted they be reunited with the rest."

They walked on, the silence only broken by the sound of birdsong. As they approached the lake where they could see Clarice and the young earl deep in conversation, Helen looked up and said, "Please, sir, I ask you not to reveal what I have told you."

James looked into her eyes. "Of course. May I say that your story brings you nothing but my admiration. You have survived and thrived where many would have given up all hope."

Helen's reply caught in her throat as Clarice came toward them. "You have been inordinately slow. Redcar and I have already walked round the lake. Now on the way back to the carriage, you must tell me about your estate in Yorkshire, Lord James. Redcar tells me it is one of the finest grouse moors in the country." She put her arm through his, leaving Helen to walk with the earl who regaled her with stories of his travels through Europe. She nodded politely at what she hoped were the appropriate points, but she heard not a word.

As James handed them down from the carriage he said, "I apologize, ladies, I must take my leave, I have an appointment at court. I shall send the carriage back for my mother." He bowed over Clarice's hand. "A pleasure, Lady Clarice."

He took Helen's hand, rubbing his thumb over it before bending to kiss it. "It has been a most enlightening afternoon, Miss Rockingham, and I hope to continue our conversation another time."

CHAPTER 5

"*I* have never been more ashamed and embarrassed in my life. Though why I should feel ashamed, I do not know. You are the one who should feel ashamed, you have polluted the fine blood and name of this family." Lady Eunice had wasted no time in berating Helen once Clarice had described the call and ride. "No wonder his lordship made an excuse to leave."

"He left because he had an appointment at court," Helen defended herself.

"He left because your behaviour was embarrassing, discussing ridiculous books and flirting with him when we were out," Clarice put in. "I shall never forgive you if you have ruined my chances of a match. Never." She ran from the room in tears, whether of anger or upset, Helen was unsure.

Lady Eunice turned to her. "Let me be clear on this. I never wanted you. Had my husband been out when you were delivered from the Workhouse like some unwanted parcel, you would have been put out of our house and out of our lives before he knew of your existence. For many years, I have fed you, clothed you, treated you as one of the family, and this is how you repay my charity. You will not go to the Queen's Masquerade tomorrow, I refuse to allow it. You will stay here and consider your improper behaviour. You will go to your room until further notice when we shall continue this discussion. I am too angry to discuss this further now, but this conversation is far from over."

Helen hung her head and walked toward the door but turned when she heard, "Let me warn you, miss, if there is another incident, no matter how small, that I judge to bring the family name into disrepute, you will be sent back to Yorkshire. I shall not let you disgrace us." Lady Eunice turned away as Helen quietly closed the door.

Hours later, when Helen heard the rest of the family go out, she ventured down to the drawing room. She sank onto the sofa. She had always known that Lady Eunice had merely tolerated her presence. She was only ever distantly polite, better when Uncle William was present, but this tirade confirmed what Helen had long suspected—that not only did Lady Eunice not like her, she actually hated her.

As a child, Helen had always tried to be good and obedient, it had been drummed into her of her great good fortune to be brought up as a lady. In the early years, Lady Eunice had enjoyed the admiration and compliments that raising an orphan had brought her. Helen had been sent to the same school as Clarice and worked hard. It had been made clear that an education cost money, though it had not seemed to inspire her cousin to academic achievement.

Clarice had been at the centre of a group of girls who paid little attention to their studies. They had also been a group of girls who exercised huge influence on others. Anyone who showed an inclination to be friendly toward Helen had been given the cut direct until eventually girls stopped trying. If they were friends with Helen, they would have no other friends.

Helen had taken refuge in books and writing and had left the school as its best ever student. "Such a shame women are not permitted to go to university, my dear," the headmistress had said as she left.

Naturally, her academic achievements were little recognized. "Helen fancies herself as some sort of bluestocking," Clarice had sneered one afternoon as the three women sat in the drawing room.

Lady Eunice had looked up from her embroidery. "Now, do not be unkind, dear, Helen will not have the advantage of making a brilliant match, given her unfortunate background. She must make her own way in the world, so a position of governess may be possible." She had turned to Helen. "Yes, my dear, a good education and the manners you have learned here should make it entirely possible that you could become a governess possibly even to one of the great families. In fact, I shall enquire among my friends to see if they are in need of a good servant."

She had spoken with a smile, but her words left Helen in no doubt. Lady Eunice had done her duty and wanted her off her hands. The earl had once again come to the rescue, insisting that both girls have their season together.

With this on her mind, Helen tucked her legs under her and took refuge in a book, her exile to her room was soon over when the earl had returned from his club. Being sent back to Yorkshire was no great punishment, being in society was. The endless calls, cups of tea, mind-numbing conversations about what people had worn last night, what they were wearing now, and what they were going to wear tonight, whether a bonnet should have ribbons or feathers, or how low a neckline could be until a girl was considered fast. Or the endless discussion of the young ladies and their admirers, who had been sent flowers, who had received poems written about them, which young men had requested a lock of hair. Not once had a young lady ever mentioned an original thought or a book she was reading, definitely not to Helen's knowledge, and possibly ever.

Her mind wandered back to Lord James. Had he been flirting with her? She could not deny that she felt a strange restlessness when he was near, or when he held her in his arms as they danced, she had not wanted to stop. Even now, just thinking about him made her feel breathless, but it was pointless. Now that he knew of the circumstances of her birth, he would want nothing more to do with her. A man who would one day become a duke would choose his wife carefully, and a woman whose grandfather was the manager of a mine was not the woman he would choose, regardless of his fine words this afternoon.

Helen sighed. Perhaps she should accustom herself to becoming a governess. She liked children, and for the most part they seemed to like her, but she knew in her heart that she wanted to write. It was possible. Miss Austen and Mrs. Burney were published authors, but was she good enough? Her teachers had thought so, but was that sufficient? Aunt Eunice would no doubt consider it to be yet another way in which Helen would bring disgrace on the family.

Her reverie was interrupted as the door was flung open. "My, but it's cold. Typical of an English summer. What are you doing in here, skulking in the dark? Come here, child, and give your grandmother a kiss." The Dowager Countess of Rockingham burst into the room, her skirts rustling behind her as the familiar scent of lavender enveloped Helen.

"Grandmama!" she squealed, throwing herself into the old woman's arms. "I did not know you were coming to London. What a lovely surprise."

"Frankly, my dear, I was getting a little bored stuck in the country and I could not resist the opportunity to see how my two granddaughters were enjoying their season." The old lady smiled. "I also wanted to catch up with the latest scandal and gossip. What is the point in being a member of the ton if one does not know what is going on?" The smile became a grin. "Now, order some tea and you can tell me about the balls and soirees you have been to, and who has offered for whom," she said as she settled herself on the sofa.

"*A*nd the Westcott ball?" the dowager asked as she sipped her tea. "I have not yet heard you mention a single young man by name? Surely at least one must have caught your eye?"

"Grandmama, you know as well as I that there is no chance of a match."

"I fail to see why. Your grandfather was an earl," the old woman said firmly.

"But my mother's father was the manager of a coal mine, that is all that people will be concerned about," Helen replied softly.

The dowager's eyes filled with tears. "I shall never forgive myself for not doing more. Your grandfather was wrong to dismiss your father from our lives. Eventually, he came to regret his actions but by then it was too late."

Helen patted her grandmother's hand. "Please, Grandmama..."

"It has to be said, my dear, we had no idea that your father was living so near to us. Had we known, your grandfather would have tried to put things right, but he died without being able to apologize. Still,"—she wiped her eyes firmly—"at least we have you, my dear. Your father would have been so proud of you. You remind me very much of him." The old woman straightened her spine. "Well, there is no use dwelling on things we cannot change. Let us talk of happier things, tell me about the costumes for the Queen's Masquerade."

Helen smiled. "The Earl and Countess of Rockingham are to go as Henry VIII and Good Queen Bess."

"Well, William certainly has the stomach for it," the dowager said and laughed. "And Eunice has the ambition."

"Clarice is to go as Lady Jane Grey."

"An interesting choice, though of course that story did not end well."

There was a pause before the dowager prompted, "And you, my dear, what are you to go as?"

"Well, as the theme is 'Kings and Queens,' I was to go as Titania, Queen of the Fairies."

"I do not understand. What do you mean you were to go?" the dowager asked sharply.

"I am afraid I rather blotted my copybook when the Marquess of Woodville called on Clarice yesterday, so Aunt Eunice says I may not attend in case I should disgrace myself further," Helen admitted.

"The Marquess of Woodville? Is he not the younger Tremaine boy, brother to the Duke of Whitney? Now heir to the Duke of Bainbridge?" her grandmother asked.

Helen nodded.

"And how exactly did you disgrace yourself? Not by putting a toad in his breeches, or a spider in his teacup, or any of the disgusting things you used to do as a child," the dowager replied crisply.

Helen laughed. "No, I believe I just distracted his attention from Clarice."

"Ah," the dowager said nodding. "Clarice has never appreciated being anything other than the centre of attention, especially where eligible young men are concerned." She looked at Helen. Her sharp eyes missed little, and though Eunice had always behaved impeccably when she was present, the dowager suspected her behaviour toward Helen was not always so sanguine. However, she had no evidence and Helen herself had never said anything to confirm her suspicions.

Helen took a deep breath. "Well, anyway, Aunt Eunice has decided that as punishment for my forward behaviour, I am not to go to the masquerade."

The dowager raised her eyebrows. "And how precisely did you distract this young, and if I may say so, extremely eligible young man from Clarice?"

"I talked to him about a book I am reading," Helen replied evasively, sure that Lady Eunice would disapprove of the book but not entirely sure what her grandmother might think.

The older woman laughed. "A book? The marquess was distracted by you talking about a book? No wonder Clarice was as mad as a cat. She would never have considered reading as a way of attracting a husband." She wiped tears of laughter from her cheek. "Though I will wager, she is at this moment in the library, trying to find a volume to match the colour of the ribbons on her bonnet. What book, pray tell, caught his lordship's interest?"

"It was the work of Mrs. Mary Wollstonecraft on the status of women," Helen said quickly.

The dowager raised an eyebrow. "I am surprised Eunice has approved that particular writer, though," she added, "seeing your rather guilty countenance, I rather imagine the works of Mrs. Wollstonecraft are something of a closed book to my daughter-in-law and should remain so."

Helen breathed a sigh of relief. This conversation with her grandmother was not turning out at all as she had imagined.

"And do you like this young man? Lord James Tremaine?" her grandmother asked.

"Yes, I do," she admitted. "Though I know nothing can come of it. He was probably just being polite."

Her grandmother smiled. "The fact is, if that young man was seriously interested in Clarice, he would not have been distracted if you had stripped naked and danced a jig in front of him."

"Grandmama!" Helen could not keep the scandal from her voice.

The old woman laughed in a way that Helen could only describe as a cackle. "One of the delights of being old is being able to shock the young. Now, I fully intend going to the masquerade and you shall come with me."

"What about Aunt Eunice? She was most definite..." Helen began.

"Leave Eunice to me." The dowager rose. "I have two advantages over Eunice, one is the fact that I am the daughter of a duke whereas she is the daughter of a knight."

"And the other?"

"I am her mother-in-law."

"But what about a costume, what will you wear?"

"Oh, I think that's quite obvious, my dear."

There was a slight pause before she added, "Boadicea."

CHAPTER 6

*J*ames leaned against the marble pillar sullenly. This was usually the sort of event he avoided like the plague, but at least a masked ball gave him a degree of anonymity. The ambitious mamas and their equally ambitious daughters had no idea which title hid behind which mask, and many of the young men were making the most of it.

Not that he was sure which particular king he was supposed to be, his sister-in-law had flung the costume at him with the words, "One of the Henrys, not the one with a penchant for changing his wives, the one Shakespeare wrote about, 'Cry God for England, Harry and St. George.'" If it was Henry V and he had to fight a battle in this dress, James thought, it is a wonder England was not yet ruled by a king named Louis and we were all speaking French. He was hot, uncomfortable, and he had to admit, more than a little annoyed—in fact he was furious.

Somehow, amongst all the throng, he had seen Helen. He'd known her despite the mask she wore. When he heard her glorious, husky voice, he felt his body stiffen. She was in the middle of a group of mostly young men who were laughing at something she said. None of them could take their eyes off her, looking ethereal as she did, standing out in silk among the rich heavy velvets and brocades most of the other women were wearing. It seemed almost as though she could fly using the small gauze wings that were attached to her waist. Her gown was the finest gossamer blue silk shot through with silver thread so that any slight movement made it shimmer. In certain lights, it almost looked as though you could see through it. He did not know whether she was aware of it, but he knew for a damn fact that every red-blooded man in the room was acutely attuned. Her hair was piled high with cornflowers and pearls threaded through the chestnut curls with one long tress curling over her shoulder. He wanted to twist it round his fingers, release all of it from the pins and let it cascade round her shoulders so that he could run his fingers through it, feel it against his lips.

He almost growled out loud as he watched her take to the floor with Sir Oliver Peyton, a libertine of the highest order, and his hand was already drifting toward Helen's pert derriere. It had been like that all evening, damnation; men were almost forming a queue to dance with the mysterious fairy queen.

"Here you are, brother," Robert said and held out a brandy snifter. "I finally discovered where the proper alcohol is kept. How women drink the punch is completely beyond me, even my dog would turn his nose up at it." There was a pause as they both drank.

"Ah, I see where your eye falls." Robert Tremaine followed his brother's line of sight. "Could this be the comely Miss Nobody who has attracted your attention?"

James did not take his eyes from Helen, who was now dancing with the heir to an earldom. "She is the daughter of the disgraced son of the late Earl of Rockingham. There was some scandal about her mother at the time." Helen had entrusted him with her story, he would not betray her trust even to his brother. Everything he had just said was already common knowledge, though he doubted that those who knew the story actually connected it to Helen.

"If everyone whose parents had a questionable past were kept from society, the ballrooms of London, Bath, Brighton, and Oxford would be completely empty," his brother observed drily. "By the by, I heard on my way through the crush that it is Lady Clarice Rockingham who is expecting one day to wear a duchess's coronet. Yours, to be precise."

"What? I have no interest in Lady Clarice."

"I assure you, I heard it from an impeccable source." He grinned.

"Who?"

"Lady Clarice herself."

Robert could not help but laugh at the horrified look on his brother's face.

"The fact is you danced with her and paid her a call. Young ladies tend to consider these things as courtship."

"I was merely being polite. I danced with a number of women, and I called to see Miss Rockingham, but Clarice clung like a barnacle on a fishing boat."

This was not entirely true, he had managed a few glorious moments alone with her, but it was not enough. He wanted her like he had wanted no other woman, even Arabella, and his brain froze at the thought. He now recognized that what he'd had with Arabella had been an immature love. With Helen he felt a need not only to make love to her, but to claim her so that she was his alone. Even more, he wanted to cherish and protect her. Was he falling in love with her? Or was his attraction to her merely physical? Whenever he thought of her, he felt desire—that he could not deny—but was it possible that his feelings could run deeper?

His brother shrugged. "Nevertheless, Lady Clarice and her mother are convinced that you are about to offer for her."

"This is ridiculous," James muttered. "I have spent less than an hour in her company and it seems I am halfway to the altar." He stopped, remembering Helen's words about lionesses and hunting. "Excuse me."

"What on earth did you say to James to send him off in a huff?" Emily asked her husband as she approached.

"Nothing, my love, James is merely contemplating becoming a monk I think," he said and laughed.

---

*B*alls are an entirely different affair when one is not sitting at the side with the older ladies, Helen thought, as she slipped down the corridor. She smiled at the thought that half the young men she had danced with had no idea who she was. They had certainly not connected her with the girl who constantly stood in the shadow of Lady Clarice Rockingham.

When she had arrived, she had done as her grandmother suggested —entered alone and had herself announced as Titania, Queen of the Fairies. It had taken most of the evening for Clarice to realize who she was, and it was only because she had exchanged a few words with her grandmother that her cousin recognized her. Within moments, the countess was bearing down on her and she decided to make her escape. She would face her aunt in the morning.

Finding a place to hide for a moment or two was not difficult, the place was huge, corridors swept in every direction. She was sure that overnight guests would have to unravel a ball of twine to find their way back to their rooms at the end of the evening. She tried two doors before finding one that was unlocked and slipped inside.

Helen could not have chosen a better hiding place had she tried. She had found the library. *In fact*, she thought, as she took more steps, *I could hide in here forever*. Her uncle's library was considered to be one of the best in Yorkshire, but this must be the best in London. Books rose from floor to ceiling like great cliffs on either side of her. Apart from the marble fireplace and windows, every wall was covered in books. There was a ladder to reach the topmost shelves and plenty of sofas and chairs on which to enjoy reading. The room was dim, lit by two small candelabras on the mantelpiece and two more on small tables.

For several moments, Helen stood drinking in the view and enjoying the smell of leather and paper before moving to the nearest shelf. She would not attempt to touch the books that were behind glass, as clearly, they were too valuable. But surely no one would mind if she leafed through some of the other volumes.

As she traced her fingers along the leather spines, she was completely unaware she was being observed. James, having dispensed with his costume for a comfortable linen shirt and trousers, had been sitting in one of the wing chairs by the fire, a glass of brandy in his hand. When the woman who dominated his waking thoughts and disturbed his dreams crept into the room, he did not know whether to thank or curse the gods of fate who had brought her to him. He knew he should make his presence known so that one of them could leave before she was ruined by being found alone with a man, and a half-dressed one at that. Yet he could not; he wanted to feast his eyes on her for a little while longer. She looked up at the topmost shelves and pulled the ladder toward her. Within seconds, she had shinned up the ladder and was leaning to reach a large volume. He frowned. She was reaching too far.

"Miss Rockingham." As he said it, the book slipped from her grasp and the ladder went in the opposite direction.

As the ladder crashed, he leapt forward and caught her. A moment later and she would have fallen, and the thought of her lying injured filled him with fear. If he had not been there, she could have broken her leg or worse and no one might have missed her for some time. "What the devil do you think you were doing? You could have broken your neck," he snapped.

"I was perfectly all right until you spoke and distracted me," she shot back. "I confess I know little about the etiquette of climbing ladders, but I am certain that distracting a person when they are up one is considered neither sensible nor polite."

"Are you injured?"

She raised an eyebrow. "No, I am perfectly all right, I should think you are more likely to be injured, sir, placing yourself under a falling object."

"I was hardly catching a runaway boulder." He grinned, the tension leaving his body. "It would certainly not have so pleasant an effect on me."

Helen turned her head. "I thank you for the assistance, but if you would be so kind as to put me down."

He relaxed his hold and she slid her feet to the ground, but he kept his arms around her. God, it felt good to hold her.

"In any case..." she went on. "Women are not made of china, we do not break so easily."

"And I am not made of stone," he muttered, crushing her to him. Every cell in his body jangled with awareness of her. "My God, you are not wearing stays," he gasped.

Helen looked at him, her eyes wide. "The modiste said they would ruin the line of my costume," she whispered.

"She was right," he replied as his lips descended. "Let's hope they are not the ruin of both of us."

Helen had been kissed before, but stolen kisses from young boys had in no way prepared her for James' sensual onslaught. Had he not been holding her, she would swear she would have melted like a candle. His tongue and lips teased as her mouth opened and he deepened the kiss, his hands roamed her back, cupping her bottom and pressing it to his hard length. She could not stop her arms snaking around his neck and her fingers from burying themselves in the dark hair at the nape of his neck, entrapping him. She almost cried out in disappointment when his mouth left hers, but a second later, his tongue swirled around her ear as he whispered, "You are so beautiful, I want you, Helen." Her head dropped back as he placed tiny kisses down her neck to the bodice of her gown. "I want to see you," he muttered, his fingers going to the fine fabric that skimmed the crest of her breasts. His fingers dipped inside and found the tips had already hardened. His thumbs circled first one and then the other as he pressed her soft body against him.

Something in his brain stirred when he heard her low moan. If he did not stop now, he would not be able to stop at all, and he knew that Helen would not stop him. She was an innocent, she did not know fully what was happening to her. Suddenly, he stepped back and placed his hands firmly behind his back. "I apologize, Miss Rockingham. That should not have happened. I suggest you leave now before you are missed, and someone comes looking for you. It would not do for us to be found alone together." *Particularly if they had witnessed the last few moments*, he added silently, still furious with himself for his near loss of control.

Helen could only look at him in shock. How could he kiss her so passionately one moment and dismiss her like a servant the next? She walked toward the door like an automaton, determined that he should not see the hurt his sudden rejection had inflicted. Clearly, he saw her as a trifle, a plaything to amuse him until he made his choice of bride. At the door she turned and said coldly, "I thank you for your company, Lord Woodville, it has been most educational."

The corridor was not empty. "There you are, Mama has been looking all over for you," Clarice's voice was shrill. "You are to go straight home. Once again you have managed to bring disgrace on yourself."

Helen nodded. Clarice was more right than she imagined.

The journey home was conducted in almost total silence. Helen could almost feel the anger emitting from her aunt as she sat, stiff-backed against the squabs. Fortunately, her uncle, oblivious as ever to his wife's moods, snored quietly. "You will go straight to bed, Helen," her aunt commanded as the coach stopped. Helen needed no further bidding; there would be trouble enough in the morning.

CHAPTER 7

The flowers arrived just as they were finishing breakfast—white roses. Clarice jumped up and took the card. "White roses, how unusual, I should have expected red."

"I believe the flowers are for Miss Helen, your ladyship," Dean, the butler intoned.

Helen looked up. "For me?"

Clarice flung the card across the table. "Apparently so, though who would be sending flowers to you I cannot imagine."

Helen broke the seal. "Yorkshire roses for a Yorkshire rose."

"Dean, take the flowers and put them in the small drawing room," Lady Eunice ordered. "Now, young lady," she added. "Hand over the note."

Helen hesitated a moment before replying, "No, Aunt, I beg your pardon, but the note is for me." She folded the note and placed it in in her pocket.

There was a moment of silence before Lady Eunice replied, "Leave the room, I do not wish to see you, ungrateful, disgraceful girl. Get out of my sight."

Helen rose and bobbed a curtsey. "As you wish, Aunt." It was the first time she had stood up to the older woman.

Clarice caught up with her on the landing. "Do not think that you will ever become Lord Tremaine's marchioness. He may take you for a carriage ride and send you flowers, but he will never marry you. He may even bed you, God knows you have given him enough encouragement. I know he was with you in the library at the masquerade, and the only reason I have not spoken, other than to Mama, is because it would ruin me to be associated with you. No one of quality will marry you, the daughter of a miner. No man would want to contaminate his bloodline with one such as you," she hissed.

Helen turned to face her. "That is enough, Clarice," she said quietly.

Clarice's face was contorted with anger. "I shall be the one to marry Lord Tremaine, our mothers have virtually agreed it, and when I am married, you may rest assured you will not be received by us or anyone else. You are a nobody and shall remain so."

Helen's eyes flashed. "Then I wish you luck, Clarice, but if Lord Tremaine intended to offer for you, I wonder why it was me he was kissing in the library and why it was I he chose to walk with when we went to the park?"

Clarice flew at her, her hand raised, but Helen caught her arm. "How dare you? Clarice screamed. "My mother should have left you in the Workhouse where you belonged, with your whore of a mother."

"Do not speak of my mother like that, ever again." Helen released her hold and Clarice pulled away.

"You have not heard the last of this," Clarice said as she stalked down the corridor.

Moments later, without conscious thought, Helen found herself walking through Belgrave Square. Her aunt had not sent her to her room, nor had she forbidden her to go out, and after the incident with Clarice, she felt in need of fresh air. It was, without doubt, a daring thing to do. A young lady never went anywhere without a chaperone of some sort, something Helen considered to be ridiculous. Adult women were treated at best as fragile dolls, too weak and insensible to take care of themselves, and at worst as infants, incapable of making rational decisions.

The freedom felt exhilarating. Before long, she found herself walking down Piccadilly, recognized the route, and decided she would visit Hatchard's Bookshop as it was not much further, and she had been many times with her uncle in his carriage. Before long, she realized she was lost. She had somehow wandered off Piccadilly, the familiar streets were no longer familiar, the buildings were crowded together, taverns and shops were cheek-by-jowl, costermongers shouted out their wares, and the fruit and vegetables were nothing like anything she had seen at her uncle's table. Narrow, dark alleys led away from the street where men and women leaned against the walls and ragged children ran about. Some sat silently, their eyes huge in their thin faces. Several times she was almost pushed into the road as people shoved and jostled.

She started as someone tugged at her sleeve. "You lost, miss?" The owner of the voice was perhaps twelve years old, though it was impossible to tell.

"I wanted to get to Hatchard's Bookshop in Piccadilly, but I seem to have missed my way," she admitted.

"I knows where it is. I could take yer if yer like."

"That would be kind."

"It will cost yer sixpence," he said and held out his hand.

Helen smiled. "And I shall be happy to pay it when we arrive."

He grinned back. "Follow me then."

As they walked, threading their way through the back streets, the boy, Charlie, told her that he was one of five brothers and sisters, his mother had died when his youngest brother was born, and he liked to keep out of the way of his new stepmother. He tried to make a bit of money running errands, but the minute he was old enough he was going to enlist in the army. As they reached the bookshop he asked, "What's it like, readin'? I never learned. I seen them squiggles, but they dun mean nothin'."

Helen thought for a moment. In truth she had never considered people like Charlie before, but she suddenly realized that had she not been taken in by her uncle, she would be just like this grubby boy, scrabbling around for something, anything that might bring in a bit of money. "Reading is a way of finding out things and sometimes seeing another kind of life."

Charlie pursed his lips and nodded. "Well, I reckon I will 'ave to get by without it now. Readin' isn't for the likes o' me."

Helen put her hands on his shoulders. "Reading and writing is for everyone. Charlie, you are a bright young man and if you had been born in different circumstances, you would have learned to read without question. Now, Mr. Hatchard is a particular friend of mine. If I can persuade him, would you want to learn to read?"

"I would, miss."

"Then wait here."

Within seconds of the shop bell ringing, Helen had spoken to young

Mr. Hatchard and arranged for Charlie's lessons. Miss Rockingham was a good customer and young Mr. Hatchard looked forward to her visits.

"There, it is arranged. You are to come here at eight o'clock sharp in the morning and in exchange for doing a few jobs, Mr. Hatchard will give you lessons." She held out her hand. Charlie wiped his hand down his shabby trousers, shook her hand, and said, "Thank you, miss." He paused before prompting, "Yer did say a sixpence."

"Of course." Helen fished a coin out of her reticule.

"I would 'ave brought yer for tuppence."

"And I would have paid a shilling."

Charlie looked at the coin in his hand. "This is a sovereign, miss."

"Use it wisely, Charlie. Do not waste your talents. Let us hope it is the start of your fortune." Helen smiled as she disappeared into the shop.

*J*ames could not believe his eyes. He could swear he had just seen Miss Helen Rockingham shaking hands with a street urchin outside Hatchard's. Had his meeting with the Austrian banker not finished early, he would have missed her.

He crossed the road and peered through the window. He did not like the sight that met him. Her bonnet was on the counter and she was laughing at something the young assistant said as they both leaned over a book. It was clear that they knew each other well, it was also clear to him that the young assistant's attentiveness was more than a wish to give good service to a valued customer. When he patted Helen's arm, James strode into the shop letting the bell ring loudly.

"Ah, Miss Rockingham, what a pleasant surprise," he said as he forced his features into a smile.

Helen turned in surprise. "Lord Tremaine, indeed, a pleasant surprise." She smiled. "Mr. Hatchard and I were looking at some books he will use to teach Charlie to read. We rather think *The Tale of the Blue Dragon* will take his fancy. What do you think?" She held out the book for his inspection.

James released the breath he had been unaware he was holding. He looked at the book. "I remember reading this as a lad, but any book about pirates is bound to go down well with any boy. Who, by the way, is Charlie?" he enquired.

"Charlie's a young boy I met on my walk this morning," Helen explained. "Mr. Hatchard has kindly agreed to teach Charlie to read in exchange for him doing some jobs." Helen turned and smiled at the young man.

"Happy to oblige, Miss Rockingham."

James could barely contain his jealousy. He was being ridiculous. Why should Helen not smile at the man? Even when he had thought himself in love with Arabella, he had never felt jealous by meaningless social exchange.

"Most commendable," he replied with as much grace as he could muster. "Perhaps if you have finished your shopping, I might escort you and your chaperone home?"

"I have no chaperone today, my lord," Helen said and smiled. "I walked here unaided, as a man would do."

James' eyebrows rose. "You did what?"

"I walked. It is a fairly simple procedure, one merely puts one foot in front of the other." She was smiling, but James did not miss the determination in her voice. The young assistant coughed discreetly. "Begging your pardon, Miss Rockingham, but it is a good thing you met Charlie."

James looked from one to the other. "It is a good thing you met Charlie because?" he prompted.

"Oh, I took a wrong turn and Charlie helped me find my way here," Helen replied airily.

James drew in an angry breath. "Have you no sense? A young woman does not wander about the streets of London unaccompanied. Anything could have happened."

"But it did not," she pointed out.

The shop bell jangled, and a couple walked in. "Might I suggest you continue your discussion through here." Mr Hatchard indicated a door behind the counter. "I am not sure that you would want my customers to overhear."

"Thank you," James said through gritted teeth as he took Helen's arm and pushed the door open.

Although there were books piled on every surface, there were two red armchairs and a fire burning in the grate. James indicated for Helen to sit as he leaned against the desk, his long legs out in front of him.

"No, thank you, my lord, if we are to argue, I should prefer to do it face to face on an even level."

James could not help smiling in spite of his anger, as she barely reached his shoulder. "I cannot believe your aunt allowed you out without a chaperone of some sort."

"Ah," Helen replied. "In my aunt's defence, she does not know I have no chaperone. In fact, she does not know I am out at all."

James' eyebrows could physically rise no higher.

Helen returned his gaze before deciding that attack was the best form of defence. "It was your fault. You sent the roses."

James frowned. "The roses? I think you are going to have to explain what the devil the roses have to do with you going out without your aunt's knowledge, not to mention picking up waifs and strays on the way and flirting with young Mr. Hatchard."

"I was not flirting. Mr. Hatchard is as interested in books as I am. We were merely having a pleasant conversation."

"Trust me, Mr. Hatchard would walk naked over broken glass with a rose up his ar…nose if you asked," James scoffed.

Helen could not stop the bubble of laughter. "Lord Tremaine, I do not think that is the sort of thing a gentleman should say."

"I am finding it increasingly difficult to behave like a gentleman where you are concerned," he muttered.

This time it was Helen's eyebrows that rose. "Me?" she squeaked. "What have I done?"

His eyes held hers as he lowered his head. "You have bewitched me," he whispered. His lips brushed against hers, then became more demanding as his arms went around her and pulled her toward him. Of their own volition, her arms wound themselves around his neck. Helen was unaware of opening her mouth, but when James slid his tongue inside she pressed her body closer. All she wanted to do was to melt into him. She felt like a flower deprived of sun and rain, suddenly opening after a summer shower.

Dear God, if I do not stop, I am in danger of throwing her on the rug and taking her now. James suddenly stepped back, but although he loosened his hold on her, he could not entirely let her go. Remembering how their last kiss ended, Helen dropped her hands to her sides.

James traced a finger down her cheek. "What? What is it?"

Her eyes were huge. "I do not know what is happening. Your kisses make my body feel so…so strange, as though it does not respond to my brain," she answered honestly.

"And do you like the way your body feels?"

She nodded, then dropped her head so that he could not see her face. "I am not sure, I am afraid you will think me wanton. I do not think a lady should feel like this, and I am certain Lady Eunice does not."

James threw back his head and laughed, it was several seconds before he could speak. "I am sure you are right. I imagine that Lady Eunice regards bedsport with the distaste she seems to feel about much in life."

Helen was puzzled. "Bedsport?"

James shook his head. "Never mind. What did you say about roses?" he asked. A conversation about the bedroom was the last thing he wanted to engage in for now, though he looked forward to initiating Helen into the pleasures of making love. She would be a responsive and passionate lover, of that he had no doubt. That thought alone shocked him, for he had never considered the pleasure of his partners before. Then again, he had never felt this way about any woman, even Arabella, and definitely none since. He had bedded them with pleasure, a great deal of pleasure, but he had never wanted to possess them body and soul and make them weak with passion.

He did not want Helen as a willing bed partner, he did not even want her as a mistress, he realized then that he wanted her as his wife. He wanted her to bear his children and to grow old at his side. Lust, he was familiar with, it was all he allowed himself to feel since Arabella had destroyed his heart, but this was not lust. Was this love? Because if it was, it was nothing like he had ever felt before. He had given his heart to one woman and it had not been enough. Arabella had almost destroyed him. He could not go through that a second time.

"The roses?" he prompted, looking for a distraction from thoughts about how Helen's body moulded to his as though they were made for each other.

"You sent them to the wrong woman."

"I can assure you, I did not."

"My aunt and cousin seem convinced," she said wryly. "My cousin went to the trouble to explain in considerable detail."

James cocked his head to one side. "And this led to an argument which led to you leaving the house without a chaperone and somehow ending up here."

"More or less," Helen agreed. "Now I had better return."

"I will escort you."

"I rather think I am in enough trouble as it is." Helen smiled.

"Then I shall escort you as far as the square."

As Helen took his arm, he drew her hand through the crook of his elbow and held it there, where she could feel the muscles of his arm tense. She smiled. Perhaps she was not the only one whose body responded of its own volition.

James kept the conversation light until they approached the square. "I shall leave you here, Miss Rockingham...Helen. Regretfully, I have to go to Vienna on government business, but should be back in a week, two or three at the most, and when I do, I shall seek you out. I expect to see you at the Maclean Ball." He raised her hand, and instead of kissing the back of it as etiquette dictated, he turned it over and kissed her bare wrist in the space between her glove and her sleeve. "Until then, my sweet." He turned and walked back down the way they had come, frowning. It bothered him that Helen referred to herself as Miss Nobody. It bothered him that her family treated her as little more than a servant, and yet her grandfather was an earl. There was something more to the story and he intended to find out what it was.

CHAPTER 8

"*I* warned you, young woman, yet still you not only disobeyed me, you once again brought shame on yourself and our noble family. I know you were alone with the marquess, do not try to deny it. Clarice told me everything. Fortunately, she was the only one to see you sneaking out of the library a few minutes before the marquess, otherwise you would have been utterly and completely ruined." Lady Eunice was so incandescent with rage she could hardly remain still. "Well, this time you have gone too far. Your assault on Clarice cannot be tolerated."

"I did nothing of the kind," Helen shot back. "Clarice made to slap me, and I caught her hand."

"Then how do you explain the mark on her face and the torn sleeve?"

"Her sleeve was torn when I caught her hand. As to the mark on her face, I have no idea. Perhaps she did it herself."

"How dare you suggest such a thing? You are a liar. I have overlooked much of your behaviour, but this assault on my daughter I cannot and will not overlook."

"Aunt Eunice…" Helen began.

"Do not presume to interrupt me. I do not wish to hear your voice," Lady Eunice snapped. "I am no longer prepared to tolerate your attempts to sabotage Clarice's chance of a match with the Marquess of Woodville, not to mention your violence and lies. I knew when first I saw you that you would cause nothing but trouble, and I was right. No amount of beating tamed that wild spirit, and I have tried my best to do so. Well, now you have gone too far. At first light you will return to Rockingham where you will stay until I have decided what is to be done with you, but mark this, you will not appear in society again. In fact, you are more likely, given your propensity for lies and violence, to find yourself in an asylum."

"My uncle will never allow this."

The countess smiled. "Your uncle is away, he left earlier to go hunting. By the time he returns, the problem of dealing with you will be solved."

There was a pause before she added, "If you think a tumble with the marquess meant anything to him, you are sadly mistaken. Men like him —men of quality—do not marry women like you, it is high time you remembered that."

"There was no tumble with the marquess, Aunt Eunice," Helen heard herself saying. "All my life, I have tried to please you in the hope that one day you would accept me, that you might even love me, but I see it was pointless. Nothing I have ever done or said was good enough."

Her aunt looked at her with eyes that were dead and cold. There was a pause before she said, "*You* will never be good enough."

"No, Lady Rockingham, it is you who will never be good enough. You did your duty in bringing me up and I will always be grateful to you for feeding, clothing, and educating me. But where was the affection? Where was the love? I wanted to see you as the mother I could not have, I wanted to love you, but time and time again you pushed me away. Well, if I am to be sent away, send me far away so that I shall not see you again." Helen turned and left her aunt standing, open-mouthed.

It did not take long for Helen to pack her small trunk. She had few gowns, and most of the space was taken up with her books and writing materials. Her aunt had forbidden any of the servants to help her in a final act of malice, since she was, as her aunt reminded her, a nobody.

There was no farewell from the family. At first light, before most of the servants were up, Helen was in a coach travelling north, alone, without even a maid for company or assistance. Her aunt had said that the staff would be better off serving true ladies than escorting whores into exile. As she watched the streets of London fade into the distance, she could not stop the odd tear falling down her cheek.

In all honesty, she could not regret too much leaving the season, she would never be accepted by society. They would not be able to see beyond the fact that her mother was the daughter of a mining engineer. She was not one of them. She would have to make her own way in the world.

Her thoughts briefly turned to James. She would never see him again, of that she was certain. Her aunt and her cousin would make sure of it and no doubt concoct some story to ensure that he would not want to see her either. She could not contact him herself as she had no idea where to post a letter to. She brushed a tear away. Memory after memory flashed through her brain—James laughing at something she had said, slipping her foot back into her slipper, his strong arms around her, his lips urgently on hers, the feel of his hands on her body. Her breasts tingled at the thought. He had made her feel like a desirable woman, loved even, and though she knew he could never love her, it had not stopped her from falling in love with him.

Helen stifled a sob, fearing if she gave into tears, she would never stop. Her hopeless infatuation for James could never come to anything, she knew that. One day, he would be a duke and he would marry someone of impeccable breeding, and that someone could never be her. Even if her wildest dreams came true and he did offer to marry her, he would be forever tarnished by her low birth and she could not bear that.

She blew her nose and sat up straight. It was no good fretting about what could never be. She had survived worse when she was a young child and she would survive this, but she needed to think and plan, and the benefit of a long coach journey meant that she had time to do just that. She would probably end up a governess, as her aunt had suggested some time before, although she was sure the headmistress at her old school would consider her as a teacher. At least if she worked in a school, she would not come into contact with anyone from high society. When James married, she would not hear of it. Someone else would be the one he kissed, someone else would be the one to love him and bear his children. She chased the idea from her mind. She must stop thinking about him. Marrying a man who would one day be a duke was the stuff of fairy tales, not for the likes of her.

Perhaps she could try to earn her living as a writer, as some women were doing now, but would anyone ever want to read her work? Encouragement from her teachers was a long way from being a published writer, and in any case, she had not the slightest idea of how to go about things. So schoolteacher or governess it would have to be. She was sure her grandmother would help, she knew virtually all the noble families, and surely one of them needed a governess.

As she travelled north, the countryside began to change from fields of golden wheat to rolling downs, then rugged peaks. Some of the roads were little more than cart tracks and the coach bumped and jolted. The inns were smaller, but the constant hustle and bustle of the stable yards, with coaches coming and going at all hours of the day and night and the blowing of the horn to announce their arrival, meant that Helen got very little sleep.

After four days, Helen recognized the cobbled market square of Richmond, and knew she was getting close to Rockingham Castle. When the coach stopped in Rockingham village and the door was opened, she was surprised to see the coachman unloading her few items of luggage from the roof.

"Why have we stopped here?" she asked.

"My orders are that you are to be left at the Dower House, miss," he grunted as he hefted her small trunk on to his shoulder. "Her ladyship, the dowager, is still in London and you are to stay here."

"Why am I not staying in my own room at the castle?"

"I could not say, miss, I was just told to bring you here."

The door to the Dower House was opened and Gillott, her grandmother's butler, beckoned her forward. "Your room is ready, Miss Helen."

"I do not understand, Gillott, why I am not to stay at the castle?"

Gillott looked uncomfortable. "Our orders are that you are to stay here until a cottage is to be made ready for you." He hesitated.

"And?" Helen prompted.

"Her ladyship, the Countess Rockingham, orders that you are not to attempt to enter the castle," he said in a rush.

"I see. I am to be banished even from my home." Helen nodded, trying to take in her new circumstances.

Gillott looked embarrassed. "I am sorry, Miss Helen, but her ladyship was most specific. Mrs. Gillott and I will do everything we can to ensure that you are comfortable while you are here."

Helen gave a small smile. "I am sure you will, Gillott. Is my grandmother expected home soon?" Surely her grandmother could not be a party to this.

"I believe her ladyship is staying in town until the end of the season and then visiting her sister in Brighton."

"Does my grandmother know I am to stay here?"

"I could not say, Miss Helen. My orders came from the Countess." There was a pause before he added, "I believe the Countess wants you settled in your own cottage before her ladyship the dowager returns."

CHAPTER 9

*A*s he was announced, James' first thought was to seek out the Earl of Rockingham and offer for Helen, so he smiled politely as Lady Maclean enquired about his trip to Vienna. Lord John was an ex-ambassador and they had many mutual connections there. Inwardly, James sighed in frustration, but good manners and their long friendship dictated that he greet his hostess with the utmost respect.

He had returned as soon as he could, unable to get thoughts of Helen out of his mind. She dominated his waking thoughts, but the dreams were torture. Every time he closed his eyes, she was there, laughing with him, dancing with him, holding out her arms for him but always just out of reach. Sometimes he dreamed she was in his bed, naked, with her hair tumbled on the pillow, but as soon as he went to make love to her, she melted away. He woke each night hot and aroused until he seemed to be in a state of permanent arousal whenever he thought of her.

Eventually, he reached the end of the receiving line and made his way toward the card room, where he was sure he would find Rockingham. The ball was in full swing and though he wanted to speak to the earl, his eyes swept the room, hoping for a glimpse of Helen. At the edge of the floor, he saw Clarice with her mother looking round and he expected to see Helen a little further back in the shadows, but he could not. Perhaps she had been sent on an errand.

"She's not here," a familiar voice spoke behind him. "When did you return?"

James turned and greeted his brother. "The boat came in on the morning tide. I had to go to the palace to make my report and here I am. Where is she?"

Robert's eyes narrowed. "The family are saying very little, just that she has been unwell for a couple of weeks and they thought she would recover better in the country air."

James frowned. "Do you believe them?" His mind was working quickly. Helen had left London just as he had gone abroad. It was no coincidence he would wager.

Robert looked at the countess and her daughter. "I could not say, but if Miss Rockingham is ill enough to be sent away, I have seen little evidence of them showing much concern."

James felt his heart clench. "They have never shown her much concern." He strolled toward the two women.

"Ah, dear Lord Tremaine, I trust your trip was successful," Lady Eunice began. "You have been sorely missed, the season just has not been the same without you."

"No indeed," Clarice echoed, fluttering her fan.

"I believe Miss Rockingham is not with you tonight?" James asked, keeping his voice light, though he wanted to shake the truth out of them.

Lady Eunice's smile slipped for a moment. "Poor Helen was taken ill almost immediately after the masquerade. We thought it best that she leave London and go to our estate in Yorkshire. Naturally, she did not want to be a burden." She smiled, but James could see that her eyes were cold.

"Poor Miss Rockingham, and what malady is it that necessitated a three-hundred-mile journey?" James asked silkily.

"Her throat."

"Her stomach."

It was Lady Eunice who tried to redeem them, saying, "Her illness started with her throat but has since affected her stomach. We felt it best that she should be isolated."

"Well, sending her to Yorkshire would certainly do that," James replied. "And has she improved?"

There was a pause before Lady Eunice turned to her daughter. "I believe I left my shawl in the supper room, please go and fetch it, Clarice."

Lady Eunice waited for her daughter to be out of earshot before she continued. "I do not wish to upset Clarice, but since you press me, Helen has been sent away to hide her shame."

James reared back, "What? Are you telling me that Miss Rockingham is with child?"

"She has brought shame on her family," Lady Eunice replied. "We had hoped to keep the matter secret within the family, but as you seem to have developed a tendre for her, it is only fair to tell you so that you know the kind of woman you are dealing with." She tapped his arm with her fan. "I am telling you this in the strictest confidence, I should not want the story to be made public and ruin Clarice's chances of a good match," she added meaningfully.

James felt as though he had been kicked in the stomach. He could not believe the Helen he knew would allow herself to be compromised in such a way. Yet her kisses had given a clue to her passionate nature, the way she had wound her arms round his neck and pressed her body against him suggested that perhaps she knew more about pleasure than he had thought. He had seen her as an innocent who did not know what she was doing. Perhaps he had been entirely wrong, perhaps she had known exactly what she was doing.

"What of the father? Is he to marry her?"

Lady Eunice shrugged. "Perhaps, if we knew who he was. Sadly, this is not the first time."

James took a breath to steady his voice. "Are you telling me that Miss Rockingham has been with other men?"

"As I said, from the moment we took her in, Helen has brought dishonour to our family, but what can one expect from one so lowborn? You are not the first young man to be taken in by her. But no matter, you need not trouble yourself that you might see her again. She has been sent away and will not return to society." She smiled. "Ah, here is Clarice."

Out of politeness, James danced with Clarice and hoped that he made the right responses to her chatter, but his mind was in a whirl. He knew from bitter experience with Arabella that women were not always as they seemed, yet he could not believe Helen was the light-skirt her aunt had suggested. Either she was the best actress in London, playing the innocent to perfection, or her aunt was lying. He turned the idea around in his mind. It was possible, if what Helen had said about her family was true, her aunt might have sent her away out of spite. When Lady Eunice was speaking, there had been no hint of affection or sorrow, just distaste. If it was indeed the case, he would travel north and find her without arousing the suspicion of Lady Eunice who would no doubt have Helen moved so that she could not be found.

He rubbed the back of his neck, and for the first time he felt unease. He did not know what he feared most—finding Helen pregnant or alone and without friends—but one thing was certain, he had to know.

CHAPTER 10

The cottage found for her was larger than Helen was expecting. There was a bedroom with a wardrobe and dressing table, a sitting room with an anteroom which she had made into a study for her writing, and a small dining room. The kitchen and scullery were at the back of the house. She had been there for several weeks and had begun to make it feel like her own home. If her aunt thought enforced solitude was a punishment, she would be disappointed, though Helen was finally grateful that her aunt clearly did not know her. Helen found the tranquility at the edge of the park useful, and without visits and calls to make, she was able to spend her days reading and writing.

Her stay in London had given her much inspiration. Every day she was up at sunrise, reading her work from the day before, rewriting and making notes, and continuing long into the night by candlelight.

When she could write no more, she walked in the park and through the woods, enjoying the dappled shade as she followed the river through the meadows. She tried to fill every moment with her work and thoughts of her work, because if not, she thought of James.

During the hours of daylight, she almost managed to banish him from her thoughts, though even then an image of his laughing eyes and full lips often came unbidden into her mind.

The nights were the worst. Every night she would toss and turn as James dominated her dreams, kissing her, his strong arms around her, she could almost feel him pressed against her. Every part of her body was alive to his touch. Her breasts tingled, her nipples hardened even at the thought of him, but as soon as she reached out to him, he faded away, and she would often wake almost crying with frustration. It was hopeless, she would never see him again.

She found taking care of the house something she enjoyed. It took up her energy as she scrubbed and polished, dusted and swept, and ensured that she went to bed exhausted, but still the dreams came. She had tied her unruly hair in a scarf and was sweeping the hearth when, one day, she became aware of a carriage drawing up in the narrow lane.

Two minutes later, her grandmother was seated on the wooden settee in her sitting room, and she was furious. "Eunice has gone too far this time, how dare she banish you? And to this, a young woman living alone in the middle of nowhere, with only the barest necessities of life?"

Helen smiled. "It is really not so bad, Grandmama. I really have all I need here. Look, I have my writing materials and time and quiet to write."

"No, Helen, it is not acceptable, and Eunice knows it. She is determined to ruin you one way or the other and I am not about to allow it. Even the servants are disgusted by her behavior. As soon as I arrived in Brighton, Gillott apprised me of the situation via a messenger. I can only apologize, my dear, that I did not come sooner."

Helen patted her grandmother's arm. "You were not to know."

"Eunice assumed that the servants were all so afraid of losing their positions without a reference that no one would tell me what was happening," the dowager went on. "However, I am back now, and you will come to the Dower House with me." When Helen opened her mouth to protest, the older woman held up a hand. "I shall accept no arguments about this, Helen, apart from the propriety of the thing, I shall enjoy the company."

Helen smiled. "Very well, Grandmama, but I should like to come here in the daylight to do some writing."

Her grandmother sighed. "Stubborn, like your father all right, but I shall send a man to stand guard and tend the garden. You will also need a maid to see to the house."

"I think the arrangement will work very well," Helen agreed, happy to be able to continue writing in peace, then frowned. "But what of Lady Eunice?"

"Eunice can go and boil her head," the dowager snapped before her expression softened. "I should have interfered years ago. The woman has bullied and harassed everyone from William and Clarice down, to get her own way. William never could stand up to her, the only one who could—" she stopped suddenly. "Well, that is over now, from now on you are my protégé. Eunice will have no further jurisdiction over you."

"I am not so sure that I want to go back into society, Grandmama," Helen admitted.

"Of course you must, how else will you land your handsome marquess?"

Helen smiled sadly. "Oh, Grandmama, I doubt that Lord Tremaine remembers my name. Besides, one day he will become a duke and would not want one such as me for a duchess."

Her grandmother's hand shot out and grasped her chin. "Look at me, child. Lord Tremaine would be honoured and proud to have you as his wife. If he has any sense at all, he will not be satisfied with a woman who merely decorates his arm and spends his money. He will want someone with whom he can talk and discuss matters other than the latest gossip and fashion." She paused before adding, "As well as someone who will keep him entertained in the bedroom."

Helen was scandalized. She did not entirely know why, there was something, some secret about what happened in the bedroom. "Grandmama, Lady Eunice said that a young lady should not talk of such things, she should not even know of them."

"Pah, I am no young lady, and Eunice is the coldest woman on earth, it's a wonder that she did not freeze William's...no matter," her eyes twinkled with amusement. "No matter, my dear, before you are married, I shall tell you what you need to know. Now go and pack your things so that we can be on our way."

*J*ames sat up straight as he sipped his tea. Compared to meeting Helen's formidable grandmother, his meetings with his associates in Vienna were like a child's tea party. It had taken several weeks to find what he wanted to know, despite the fact that his contacts in the consular service had means of obtaining information that others would find impossible.

He had counted on finding Helen at Rockingham Castle and was surprised to find she was living with her grandmother at the Dower

House. He was furious to hear of the original plan for Helen to live alone in a cottage on the estate. He had no doubts as to who had come up with that plan, but fortunately, the Lord and Lady Rockingham were not expected back from London for another week and by then, he hoped to have resolved his feelings for Helen.

The old lady looked at him in silence before asking, "What are your intentions toward my granddaughter? Just because her mother was of low birth does not mean that she will become your mistress."

James almost choked. When he had recovered himself, he put his cup down. "I can assure you that my intentions are entirely honourable, my lady."

"Pah, I am too old to fall for that one, young man. Since Adam was a lad, men have been promising honourable intentions and then being the ruin of many a girl."

"If what I hear is true, it would appear that Miss Rockingham is one of their number," he heard himself saying. "That being so, I am prepared to make her a generous offer."

The dowager's eyes narrowed. "What exactly are you saying, Tremaine? You believe Helen to be with child?"

He nodded slightly. "I have it on the highest authority."

"And you believe this?"

"I have not seen Lady Helen to ask her, nor has anyone else denied the story, as it is not uncommon"—he went on, watching her closely —"for young ladies to disappear to the country 'for their health,' I believe. Is this perhaps the case with Lady Helen?"

"Helen has no title," the dowager shot back, but James could see a gleam of interest in her eye.

"Ah, but she has," he said and then clamped his lips together. If the old woman wanted to know, she would have to ask.

"Go on."

"I have certain, ah, contacts in quite high places," he explained, "and it seems that although your husband threatened to disinherit your older son…"

"Jonathon."

"Jonathon, exactly. He never actually followed through with his threats in law."

There was a pause before the dowager spoke, "Are you saying that although Jonathon thought he was disinherited, he actually died as heir?"

James nodded.

"And in that case, Helen, as his daughter, is in fact the Lady Helen?"

"I believe so."

Her thin fingers grasped his arm and he could see tears in her eyes. "You do not know how much this means, not to poor Jonathon, it is too late for him, but for Helen's sake, this changes everything."

He smiled. "Of course, it means that Lady Helen can take her rightful place in society."

The old lady's lips twitched. "It means much more than that, young man. If Helen can be persuaded to take the title."

James frowned. "I am not sure I follow your ladyship."

The dowager's smile widened. "There is no reason why you should, young man, but all will be revealed in the fullness of time."

James shook his head, not entirely sure that the old lady was in full command of her faculties, but not wanting to risk asking. "I came here in the hope of finding out the truth about Lady Helen," he started.

"Do you love her?" the dowager interrupted.

He took a deep breath. "I intend to ask her to be my wife." He had not said it out loud before, even to himself.

"With respect, Lord Tremaine, that is not an answer to the question I asked. Marriage among those of rank is rarely based on love. Helen has had little love in her life so far, and I do not intend that she be trapped into a loveless marriage."

"I can assure your ladyship that I have the highest respect for Lady Helen and as my wife she would want for nothing, even if she is to bear another man's child."

There was a long pause while the old lady regarded him through her lorgnette before she finally said, "Nothing you have said so far, Lord Tremaine, gives me confidence that you are the right man to make Helen happy. Respect and material comfort are not acceptable substitutes for love and affection. Neither is marrying out of a sense of duty or charity."

If there were any lingering doubts that the dowager had lost some of her faculties, they were now well and truly dissipated.

James rubbed the back of his neck. Her grandmother was not making this easy for him. "Perhaps if I could speak with Helen?"

The dowager tilted her head. "I am not sure that is either advisable or appropriate. When she came here, Lord Tremaine, Helen's heart was broken. She did and does her best to hide it by making herself constantly busy, she does not think I know, but at night, I have heard her weeping. I will not have her heart, or her spirit broken again."

"The last thing I want to do is to hurt her," James began.

The old woman held up a wrinkled hand. "I am sure you do not, young man, but I fear you would."

James stood and bowed. "I will see Helen, my lady. I should prefer to do it with your blessing because I know how much you mean to her but see her I shall. There are things between us that we must resolve, for both our sakes."

The door was flung open.

"Grandmama, have you seen this letter…"

---

*A*ll colour drained from her face as Helen came face to face with the man who dominated her waking thoughts and haunted her dreams. "I am so sorry, my lord. Grandmama, I had not realized you had a guest."

She started to back out of the room, desperate to leave before James saw her tears. Before she had taken three steps, he was in front of her, folding her small hand in his large one. "Please do not go," he said softly. "It was you I came to see."

She was thinner, he could see that, and there were dark shadows under her eyes which looked huge in her delicate face. Had he done that to her? He spoke the truth when he said that he would never hurt her. Clearly, she was not with child and he was disgusted with himself for being prepared to even half-believe Eunice's lies which were obviously designed to keep him away from Helen. For a man who was supposed to be intelligent, he had been a fool.

"I shall give you ten minutes alone," the dowager announced, rising to her feet. "And if you cannot resolve things in that time, Tremaine, you are not the man I think you are." She winked as she progressed to the door and closed it behind her. There was silence, broken only by the crackling of the logs on the fire.

James did not want to talk, all he wanted to do was take Helen in his arms and kiss her until she could think of nothing else. He wanted to taste her luscious lips and feel her body as she melted toward him, to feel her softness against his hard body, and—he noted—his body was hard already. She had only to walk into the room and his body responded.

However, things had to be said before anything could be settled between them. All he knew was that he would not leave this room until Helen had consented to marry him.

Finally, Helen raised her head and looked at him. "Please sit, Lord Tremaine. Should I order more tea?" She took a seat on one of the armchairs safely out of reach.

"No, thank you." His tongue felt as though it was stuck to the roof of his mouth. "I do not want tea." And he did not. He wanted her.

She smiled. "Then what would you like to say? I must warn you, if Grandmama says ten minutes, that is what she means."

He took a deep breath. For some reason, he, who had faced danger on the battlefield and negotiated for his own businesses as well as the government without a second thought, was nervous. It would be easy to omit the story of her supposed pregnancy, but he had to be honest, everything must be out in the open or they could not build a relationship of trust.

"I came partly because I was told that you were with child," he said bluntly.

Helen's eyes widened. "With child?"

"Your aunt said that you were ruined, that you had lain with a man, and that it was not the first time." He was being brutally honest, but without honesty they would never be able to move on.

Helen felt sick. "But why would my aunt say such things? Surely apart from being my ruin, they would bring the family dishonour."

"I do not believe she has made this public, I believe she only told this fable to me."

Her blue eyes pierced him. "And you believed her? I confess I am ignorant of many things, but I know that an unmarried woman who bears a child is ruined."

There was a pause before he answered, "I did not want to believe."

"But you did."

He ran his hand through his hair. "Before I answer, I must tell you something of my past. It may explain why I reacted as I did. All I ask is that you listen."

"Go on."

He took a deep breath. He owed Helen the truth, and if afterward she could find it in her heart to excuse his judgement of her character, they might have a chance. He refused to think of what he would do if she refused him, but only the truth could help him now.

He took a ragged breath. "Several years ago, I was betrothed to Lady Arabella Walmesly. I had been in love with her, or at least thought I was, since I was a young lad. She was first promised to my cousin, then to my brother, but patience and circumstances finally led her to me."

At Helen's puzzled look he explained, "You are aware how marriages work in society, Arabella's family had arranged a match between her and my cousin, Christopher, who at that time was heir to the Dukedom of Whitney. When he died in battle, Robert, my brother unexpectedly became heir. Arabella transferred her affections with little difficulty, though ambition was I think the primary motivation. She was insanely jealous when Robert fell in love with Emily and did all in her power to sabotage the match. I had loved her, or thought I had since being a boy, dazzled by her beauty I suppose, but when she fell ill, I was able to help her. I thought she returned my love, but I was mistaken, she was grateful, that was all."

He paused. James had rarely discussed this with anyone, he had barely allowed himself to think about it, even after several years the memories were painful. "Shortly before the wedding, Arabella jilted me. She had been having an affair with a man I once considered to be a friend, she had fallen in love with him and could not go through with the wedding."

He glanced up. Helen regarded him steadily, her hands folded in her lap, though her knuckles were white. "The invitations had been sent out. Arabella had always expected to make a brilliant marriage, but certain things had happened, and I now realize that she was settling for me. At the time, I was a mere second son, not expected to inherit wealth or title. Arabella and her family had come close to ruin, she needed to marry quickly, and I was a convenient solution. I did not have wealth, but I did have respectability and a title, which was enough. Anyway, when Peter came along, Arabella fell in love with him and the wealth he could provide. They went to America."

"And this is why you were prepared to believe I was with child?" Helen asked softly. "Because of Arabella's behaviour, you did not trust me?"

"I have found it difficult to trust any woman,"—his eyes held hers—"until you."

She returned his gaze. "I am not Arabella," she said firmly.

"I know that," he replied. "Believe me, I know. I can only apologize for believing the worst when nothing you have ever said or done justifies my judgement."

Helen stood up and held out her hand. "Thank you for your honesty and your apology."

James looked down at her proffered hand. She was about to dismiss him from her life and that he could not allow. He took her hand in both of his. "I cannot leave with things between us unsettled."

Helen looked into his eyes. "But things are settled, Lord Tremaine. You have apologized for your judgement and I have accepted it. You may go on your way with a clear conscience."

She did not know how she managed to keep her voice steady. In a moment he would leave the room and walk out of her life forever. Leaving London without seeing him had been bad enough, because she had thought, foolishly, that he would come for her, but now the gulf between them was so great, they would never be able to bridge it. She fled from the room before the tears started to fall.

CHAPTER 11

"*B*ut this is marvellous news," the dowager exclaimed as she looked up from the letter. "You are to become a published author, following in the footsteps of Miss Austen and Mrs. Burney. I am very proud of you."

"I would hardly place myself in the same class. Indeed, I am still at a loss as to how Mr. Thompson got hold of my work."

"I sent it to him, of course. You left behind some stories when you left London. Had I left matters to you, they would no doubt be languishing at the back of a drawer somewhere. Nothing ventured, nothing gained as they say. You really must step out from Clarice's shadow, Helen."

Her grandmother regarded her seriously before adding, "Forgive me, my dear, but you do not seem to be as delighted as I about this news."

Helen smiled. "I am, Grandmama, truly I am," she said and sighed. "It's just that…" She hesitated.

"It's just that Lord Tremaine did not come up to scratch?" As ever, her grandmother was direct.

"I thought he was different, that he saw me for what I am and that he liked me, despite everything," she admitted. When she had seen James yesterday, her heart had leapt, but his judgement of her character showed that he did not know her at all and she certainly did not know him.

"Love is never easy, child, but you will meet the man who is right for you one day," her grandmother spoke gently.

Helen sat up straight. "But things are different now, Grandmama. Now that I have a publisher, I shall be able to earn my own money and live independently. I shall not need to get married, nor do I intend to."

Her grandmother shook her head. "Well, we shall see, my dear. Firstly, you must send a message to Mr. Thompson accepting his contract, then you must call on your uncle. There was a message from the castle at first light summoning you."

"But I thought I was not allowed to enter the castle?"

"William has arrived early, alone, and wishes to see you, that is all I know."

An hour later, Helen's mind was in a whirl, as the last person she expected to see was sipping coffee in her uncle's study. Her uncle had clearly believed his wife's story that she had been sent north to recover from some malady, and it was James who had convinced him to see for himself. After enquiring about her health, he launched straight into news that shocked and astounded her.

"Well, little miss, it seems that we are to have a wedding before Christmas. The Marquess of Woodville here has offered for you. We have agreed the settlement. Lord Tremaine has generously offered to take you with a modest dowry. You are now officially betrothed," he beamed. "To think that one day, my little niece will be a duchess."

Helen sat down before her knees gave way and looked from one man to the other. Her uncle smiled broadly, James looked furious. "I do not understand, Uncle. Much as I am flattered by his lordship's proposal, I had no idea that Lord Tremaine was at all interested in a match, especially to me."

"Then you must get used to it, my dear," her uncle said airily, "as the contract has already been signed. Surely you knew that you must marry someday, and," he added, looking serious for a moment, "I doubt you would get a better offer."

James could have cheerfully throttled the earl. He was making his proposal sound like an ill thought-out business contract. He had wanted to propose properly, Helen deserved it, but now he would be lucky if she would listen to him recite a shopping list, especially after the hash he had made of their last meeting.

Helen was furious with her uncle and with James. "How dare the pair of you make an agreement about me? I am not some chattel to be bought and sold. I do not wish to marry Lord Tremaine, in fact, I do not wish to marry anyone."

The earl looked shocked. James cleared his throat. "I wonder, your lordship, if I may have a few moments alone with my fiancée," he asked.

"Of course, young man, perhaps you would care to take Helen for a stroll in the gardens. I am sure a little walk and some fresh air and she will see things quite differently. The maze is particularly fine this year."

James intended to heed the older man's advice and escorted Helen into the gardens. For several minutes they walked in silence before Helen spoke calmly, her anger now under control, "I fear there has been some mistake, my lord. I am most flattered by your proposal, but I cannot accept it. I think it would be best if you were to leave now. No one need ever know you made an offer and we can both get on with our lives without anyone being hurt."

James braced himself. "No, Helen, I cannot leave without you. I came here to ask you to marry me. I wanted to ask you yesterday, but I made such a mess of our meeting."

Her eyes widened in shock. "But you thought I was bearing another man's child."

"I was a fool to even think it, but yes, even so, I would have raised the child as my own. I did not care what you had done, though I now realize a few poisonous words in my ear nearly wrecked our chance of happiness. I love you, Helen, I have for some time, I do not know how or when it happened. If I am honest, I admit that what I felt for you at first was merely lust, but what I now feel is deeper, much deeper. I love you, body, mind, and soul. For some reason, the gods or Fate or some power brought us together that night. Please say you will marry me before I go out of my mind." He brought her hand to his lips and kissed it tenderly.

"You want to marry me? Truly?" Helen was incredulous.

"I truly do." He smiled down at her.

"And this is not some jest, or marriage of convenience?"

"It is not. I know that among the ton many marriages are arranged for reasons of amassing power and wealth, but that is not what I want. And," he said with a smile that reached his eyes, "knowing as you do that a hoard of young ladies and their mothers will be all too willing to throttle me, you cannot argue that any marriage I make will be convenient."

She froze and withdrew her hand. "I am honored, Lord Tremaine, but I cannot accept."

He reared back. "Why in the blazes not?"

She smiled sadly. "Oh, Lord Tremaine—James—surely you must know the answer. We are not of the same class. You are a marquess, one day to be a duke. As you said, there are many eligible ladies awaiting your hand. My father was disinherited, and my mother's father was an engineer in a coal mine. I am nobody. Even if we were to marry, I would never be accepted, and you would be tainted by my low blood." She sighed. "I wish it could be otherwise, but it cannot."

His blood had run cold when she spoke, but he was once again hopeful. "Are you saying that this is the only impediment to our marriage? That other than ancient family history you would consider accepting my offer?"

She nodded.

He stopped and faced her, his large hands on her narrow shoulders. "In light of what you have just said, dare I hope that you have feelings for me?"

She turned her face toward him. "I think you know that I do." There was no point in lying.

For the first time, the tension left his face. "Then I may have the solution to our problem," he whispered. His hands held her face as he lowered his head and kissed her lips, gently at first, but at her soft moan, he became more demanding. When she grasped the lapels of his jacket and stepped closer, his arms went around her, pulling her to him, moulding her body to his. He wanted her there and then, his rigid arousal demanding release, yet he knew he could not let this progress further than a kiss. James had kissed many women and bedded more that he cared to remember, but none of them managed to have the effect that Helen had on him. He was like a moonstruck boy whenever she was near, and if he did not step back soon he would not be able to, and he had no doubt that the earl would come after him with a shotgun, and rightly so. Betrothal or not, he had no right to despoil his fiancée in the middle of the maze.

He broke the kiss but kept her in his embrace. He could not help noticing that she was as breathless as he, nor did it escape him that there was hurt in her eyes. "What is the matter, sweetheart?" he asked, tracing a thumb across her swollen lips.

Helen swallowed. "I cannot deny that your kisses are...pleasant, but each time you have kissed me, you have instantly set me aside like a troublesome puppy."

"Pleasant? My kisses are only pleasant?" he growled, hauling her into his arms once more. "Damned if I will have my kisses described as merely pleasant," he muttered as he covered her mouth with his own, demanding entry, touching his tongue to hers and withdrawing, then plunging in again and again until they were both breathless. He could feel her melt against him and it almost undid him. When he stepped back this time, they were both breathless.

Helen's entire body felt as though it was aflame. While he was kissing her, she wanted to be as close to him as possible; she wanted to feel his skin on hers without the encumbrance of clothing. She wanted his hands and lips to touch her and she wanted to touch him skin to skin. She made to step back, disturbed by her thoughts, but James would not let her go. "Tell me again how it feels when I kiss you," he breathed against her ear, sending shivers down her spine.

"I feel as though I am about to burst into flames," she replied breathlessly.

He looked down at her. "That's better." He grinned. "Now that you have soothed my masculine pride, let me tell you that when we are married, I fully intend to kiss and caress every inch of your body from the top of your head to the tip of your toes, and you will like it even better than the kissing. I warn you, Helen, I want you as I have never wanted a woman before, and I believe I shall never get enough of you."

Now that he had stopped kissing her, Helen could begin to formulate a reply. "Please...Lord Tremaine, do not make this more difficult than it already is, I have explained why there cannot be a match between us. I am trying," she added, "to save you from social ruin. I am nobody and for both our sakes should remain so."

James became serious. Helen would not move on this, he knew, until her fears would be assuaged. He led her to the lovers' seat in the middle of the maze and took both her hands in his.

"Let us consider your objections. Firstly, you should know I do not give a damn about the approval of society. They can either accept us or not, but I think they will. I am related to some influential families and count others as my friends. Besides," he said, grinning, "once the society matrons begin to know you, they will be as charmed as I am."

Helen rolled her eyes but did not argue, which gave him encouragement. "Secondly, you are, in fact, Lady Helen Rockingham.

Although your grandfather threatened your father with disinheritance, he never carried out his threat in law. Even though your father predeceased his father the earl, he still died as heir though he did not know it, and you, as his legitimate daughter, are a Lady."

Helen's mouth formed a small O. "But I do not understand, why was I never told this?"

"I have a feeling your aunt had something to do with it." James' mouth formed a grim line. "I have one of my men working on the implications."

"So I am Lady Helen Rockingham?" The title sounded strange in her ears.

James smiled. "Indeed, you are my lady, and your mother…"

"Would have been a countess, had she lived," she breathed, the tears shimmering in her eyes. Although lowborn, her mother would have made a finer countess than Lady Eunice could ever be.

"Will you accept the title?"

Helen thought for a moment. "I am used to being plain Miss Rockingham. I am the same person I was before you told me, and part of me wants no part of it, however, I will accept it in honour of my mother who was a lady, title or no. Though I should like it to remain secret until I am used to the idea."

James looked at her with pride and admiration. "I believe I have now dispensed with your reservations, but the final reason I wish to wed you is that I love you, Lady Helen Rockingham, deeply and sincerely, and I wish you to be my wife, the mother of my children, and the woman with whom I wish to live out my life."

"Then yes, my lord, I shall be honoured to marry you."

"Thank God," he muttered as he took her in his arms once more.

"There is one additional problem," Helen said hesitantly as they drove back to the Dower House.

James kept his arm around her as he expertly drove the two matching bays. "What is that, my love?"

"I am to have a book published, a novel. Grandmama sent some of the pages to a publisher and he has agreed to publish my work."

James looked down at her. "And why is this a problem?"

Helen returned his gaze steadily. "Some men would object to their wives earning money in this way."

James stopped the carriage and turned to her. "Helen, I cannot raise a single objection. As a matter of fact, I shall be proud of my clever wife. I remember a conversation early in our acquaintance when you were very clear about your opinions of the education of women and their place in public life. It gave me a great deal to think about. I shall be only too happy to support your writing and not only that, I shall shout about it from the rooftops."

Helen laughed. "It is only one book, and it may not be any good."

"I doubt that, otherwise the publisher would not have taken it. I assure you, Helen, I cannot claim to know specifically about publishing, but it is a business like all others and they will be expecting to make some money from it. They do not publish books to indulge young ladies."

"It will mean that I have to devote time to it."

"Of course you will. Nothing of note ever came without effort, but that is a good thing. Helen, you will have your work and I will have mine. Again, since our conversation, I realized that, although I could leave much of my work to the excellent people I employ, I want to work, it gives my life purpose. I had not really thought of it before, but I imagine it is the same for women. In fact," he added, "I have a feeling my sister-in-law is of the same opinion."

"Yet many women have to be content with filling their days with very little because their fathers and then their husbands have not allowed them to develop the skills needed for, well, anything other than being a wife, mother, and decorative hostess," she replied.

"Fortunately for you, your husband-to-be is an extremely forward thinker, who"—he grinned—"is looking forward to being addressed as the husband of the famous novelist, Lady Helen Tremaine."

Her eyes softened. "Lady Helen Tremaine, novelist. I like that."

When they arrived back at the Dower House, her grandmother's face was wreathed in smiles as they told her of their engagement. "When is the wedding to be? I suggest at Christmas, everyone loves a Christmas wedding. It could be just before the end of the little season, before people go to their estates for the holiday, in which case it would be at St George's in Hanover Square. Of course, we could have it in the minster in York, I have known the archbishop since we were both in leading strings so I do not imagine there would be a problem. There is so much to plan."

Helen laughed, holding up her hand. "Grandmama, I have only been betrothed for a few hours, but I imagine a small ceremony here in the village would do."

"Nonsense, my dear, a society wedding with all the trimmings is exactly what is needed to launch you into society properly, and I never again wish to hear you say that something will do when it most certainly will not. Besides," she added wickedly, "I cannot wait to see Eunice's face when she sees you walk down the aisle to marry your handsome lord."

"I rather think I have the naughtiest grandmother in the country." Helen laughed. "But I think Lord Tremaine and I would like a small wedding."

"Pah…" Her grandmother sniffed. "What say you, Tremaine?"

Were he to be honest with himself, James would marry as soon as possible by special license. For an instant, he was transported back five years ago when his wedding to Arabella was to have been a large society event with the invitations sent and gifts already starting to arrive. He could hardly bear the thought of something going wrong this time. He quickly shook his head to clear the thoughts and smiled at Helen. His fears had nothing to do with her. "Lady Helen must have whatever she wants, I do not care if our wedding is huge or small so long as we are married."

"Well then," the dowager said triumphantly, "we shall need at least six months, possibly a year. These events do not plan themselves."

"We shall be married at Christmas, at the latest," James said firmly. "I have waited long enough to find the right woman. I do not intend to wait any longer."

"Very well, that's decided—though it is only weeks away—but we shall pull it off, I have no doubt. Now then, we shall be in London by the end of the week. Your uncle will announce your engagement in *The Times*, then we must visit the modiste for your wedding dress and trousseau. Tremaine, you will need to ensure that Helen is introduced into society, small events first. I give you the responsibility to ensure that she is well-received," she said sternly.

"My goodness, ma'am, should you ever consider a career in the military, I believe if you signed up in the morning, you would be made general by tea-time." James laughed.

"You would be surprised at what women can achieve, young man, when given the chance." Looking at Helen's surprised expression, she laughed. "What? You are not the only one to read Mary Wollstonecraft."

Helen suddenly became alarmed by a sudden thought. "Grandmama, who is to pay for all this?" Certainly not her aunt who had always made it clear that there would be no dowry.

"I have more than sufficient funds to pay for it, my dear, and nothing would give me greater pleasure than spending it on your wedding. I have no desire to be the richest woman in the graveyard, though." The dowager looked at James. "I think it is fair to say that from now on, instead of the hand-me-downs and cheap gowns your aunt has chosen for you in the past, you will be dressed as well as any of the women of fashion."

"But I do not need…"

James cut her off. "I know, darling, but I want you to face society without feeling at a disadvantage and although it is shallow, I believe a new wardrobe will give you some confidence. And," he added, "your grandmother is right, your aunt's choice of clothing is appalling."

Her grandmother looked from Helen to James. "I like this one, Helen. Ensure that you do not lose him. And you," she added, looking sternly at James, "if you make my granddaughter unhappy, you will answer to me."

CHAPTER 12

*J*ames' breath almost completely left his body as he watched Helen descend the white marble staircase of her grandmother's town house. No one would recognize the plain Miss Nobody he had met at the Westcott Ball from the beauty in front of him. Helen's hair gleamed in the candlelight. It was pinned up with a few soft curls at the nape of her neck and more framing her face, interspersed with sapphire pins, sparkling, and glittering as they caught the light. The modiste had done a superb job, perhaps too well. James was glad that they were only going to the opera tonight. Had it been a ball, he would have to spend the night beating other men away with a stick.

Helen's gown was of the finest silk the colour of the sapphires that adorned her hair and emphasized the extraordinary colour of her eyes. The bodice was cut so low that it skimmed the top of her breasts drawing his eyes to her soft curves. He could not help the soft moan escape his lips.

Helen's smile wobbled, and she looked anxious. "Is something wrong? Is the gown too revealing? I said as much to Grandmama, but she said it displayed my advantages to perfection."

"Your grandmama is a shrewd judge of both men and women." James laughed and held out his hand. "Is the dowager joining us?"

Helen smiled. "I am afraid not. She sends her apologies and said to

tell you that she has a headache which will not be made any better by a
'lot of squawking women'. She also suggested that, as your mother is to
accompany us, I would be well-chaperoned in any case, though why a
woman is not considered adult enough to need a chaperone is frankly
ridiculous."

James grinned. Life with Helen would be anything but dull. She
seemed to have inherited a fair degree of her grandmother's feistiness. "I
think it is to protect delicate maidens from the unwanted attentions of
predatory males."

"I can assure you that should any predatory male make the mistake
of annoying young women, he has clearly never attended a girls'
boarding school, otherwise he would think twice," she shot back.

His grin grew wider. "Words I would do well to remember." He held
out his arm, but when Helen went to take it, he pulled her into his arms
and kissed her thoroughly. "Unwanted attention of a predatory male," he
growled. "Now you know why the chaperone is needed," he added as he
released her.

"Most interesting," Helen replied. "But there is a fairly obvious flaw
in your argument."

He quirked an eyebrow.

"Your attentions are not unwanted. Now, shall we?" Helen could not
help a giggle at his bemused expression.

"God help me," he muttered as he draped the shawl around her
shoulders.

"I was beginning to think I should have to send a search party." Lady
Tremaine's words were tempered by her smile. "Good evening, my dear.
You look splendid. I imagine the gossip sheets will be full of you
tomorrow. I cannot tell you how pleased I am that James has at last
found someone to make his life complete."

"I certainly hope so," Helen responded, liking the older woman
more each time she saw her.

"Neither of my sons seem to have chosen brides who conform to
society's conventions, and I would wager, are happier for it. Now tell me
about this book James has been speaking of. I cannot tell you how proud
of you he is, as am I. Just think, a writer in the family and a woman
to boot."

The journey passed rapidly with the two women chatting happily.
James half-listened, but he took advantage of the opportunity to look at
Helen's animated face as she explained her love of writing. No wonder

her aunt had dressed her in dowdy gowns with her hair scraped back when she had appeared in society. Her creamy skin and fine features were breathtaking, her eyes sparkled, and her full mouth just demanded to be kissed. He almost groaned out loud when she suddenly threw back her head and laughed at something his mother said. He could not see the outline of her body while it was wrapped in a warm travelling rug, but having held her in his arms, he could imagine the curve of her narrow waist against the seat and full breasts which he could not wait to touch. He lost himself picturing her on their wedding night when he would slowly ease her out of her nightgown and lay her on his bed. He would first run his fingers over her skin before attending to her breasts which he would tease with his fingers until they budded, then ravage them with his tongue while his hand travelled lower.

"James." He heard his name and sat up, hoping that the evidence of his recent thoughts was not visible.

"James, cease your wool-gathering this instant, we have arrived at the Opera House," his mother chided.

"Now, my dear," Lady Tremaine said and turned to Helen. "Time for you to make your mark on society. Keep your head high, remember, most of the women have not a thought in their heads beyond the next gown or pair of slippers. You, however, have a family which includes two engineers and a writer. You have nothing to fear from any of them."

She turned to her son. "I suggest that if you are to keep your wits about you tonight, you keep your thoughts on Lady Helen's eyes. Now," she added with a twinkle in her eyes, "I furthermore suggest you close your mouth and escort us into the theatre, otherwise we shall arrive only in time for the encores."

"*A*re you ready?" James paused at the entrance to the box. He knew that once they entered, Helen would be subjected to intense scrutiny. The eyes of the ton would be on her in a way she had never experienced and possibly had not imagined. "I think so," Helen replied, her smile wobbling.

James bent to brush a kiss across her cheek. "You are the most beautiful woman I have ever known. I will be the envy of every man here. But remember," he added, his eyes glinting, "you are mine. Mine to love and protect until the day I die."

Her eyes filled with tears at his words, overcome with the realization once again that she was truly loved. "Oh, James," she whispered.

"Now stop looking at me like that, or I shall be tempted to take you back to the carriage, drive home at breakneck speed, and have my wicked way with you before the orchestra have finished the overture," he said, wiggling his eyebrows in an outrageous leer.

"Oh, James," Helen repeated, this time with a giggle.

"James, I suggest that you and Lady Helen take your seats, otherwise the performance will be over before you sit down." Lady Tremaine's voice pierced through the door, but Helen could hear amusement in her tone. They entered the box just as the lights were dimming and as soon as she sat down, James threaded his fingers through hers and squeezed her hand lightly.

"Excellent timing," he whispered as the orchestra struck up.

For the next hour, Helen was transfixed by the action on stage. She had rarely attended the theatre and had never been to the opera before.

"Of course *The Beggar's Opera* is a bit of fun being poked at some of the more fanciful operas," James whispered as the first act drew to a close.

Helen's eyes were wide. "Is it not a little risqué for young ladies of the ton?"

James smirked. "Oh, you noticed that, did you?"

"Well, one could hardly miss it. I do not imagine those 'ladies of the night' are nurses, now do you?" she shot back.

He laughed. "And are you shocked?"

"Not at all, and I can easily see that they would be attracted to Captain Macheath. Such a handsome man." She sighed dramatically.

"I suppose so, if you like that sort of thing," he said, his voice terse.

"Oh, I imagine most women do." She smiled sweetly. "That is why they cast him. You men get to ogle Polly and Lucy and we women feast our eyes on Macheath. It is only fair," she finished, her eyes dancing with mischief, waiting for his response.

"I do not think well brought up young ladies are supposed to leer at men," he responded sharply.

"I cannot see why not. Polly's gown was cut so low that when she leaned over, half the men in the stalls nearly fell off their seats. Why is it acceptable for men to look over women predatorily, but unacceptable for women to appreciate masculine beauty in the same way?" she asked, enjoying herself immensely.

He leaned forward. "When we are married, my love, you may leer at me and only me as much as you like, but be warned, there will be consequences. And," he added, grinning devilishly, "I very much look forward to your scrutiny. Now let me fetch you some refreshments to cool you down before the orchestra strikes up again, and you continue your salivating over Captain Macheath, who by the way is as bald as a coot under that wig."

As the door to the box closed, Lady Tremaine confided, "Helen, if I may call you that, I must tell you that I have not seen James so relaxed and happy for many years. No doubt he has told you of Arabella's faithlessness. From that day, he became harder in some way, as though to protect himself. He devoted himself to work and making money, I think because lack of money and position were the reasons Arabella rejected him, but none of it made him happy. You have done that. You have brought him back to life."

"Thank you, Lady Tremaine."

The older woman touched her arm. "Please do not hurt my son. For all his strength, I do not think he would recover should he face rejection again. A broken heart may mend once, but it cannot heal twice."

Helen smiled at her future mother-in-law. "James and I have made each other whole, Lady Tremaine. Rest assured that I love him with all my heart and would never want to hurt him."

Lady Tremaine's eye filled with tears as she hugged Helen. "He was so lucky to have found you, my dear," she whispered as the lights went down.

Throughout the second act, James' arm wound itself around her waist. Helen knew she should make some sort of token protest, but all she wanted was to be in his arms, in private. She wanted to feel his lips on hers, his body on hers, his hands on her breasts which were feeling heavy and warm at the very thought. She was so distracted by his warm, firm body scandalously close that she barely noticed when the curtain went down at the end of the act.

Eventually, she became aware of a buzz in the audience and that the entire audience now seemed fixated on the box opposite them. Sitting in the once-empty box was an older couple with a beautiful, golden-haired woman in an ice blue gown and flashing sapphires. "Who is that? Everyone seems intrigued by her."

When James failed to respond, she turned to him and was concerned to find that his face had lost all colour. "Are you quite well, my lord? You look as though you have seen a ghost."

"I believe I have," he murmured. "That is Lady Arabella Walmesly."

The rest of the performance was a blur as Helen's mind whirled. What did this mean for her relationship with James? Arabella had been the love of his life, he had said so. Now that she had apparently returned from the dead, perhaps he would want to return to her. No matter his protestations about how Arabella was in the past, people never forgot their first love. Perhaps even if he went ahead with their marriage, he would always be wondering what might have been, especially now that he appeared to have been given a second chance.

The newspapers were full of Lady Arabella's miraculous return. It seems she had been one of a handful to have been saved but had lost everything in the wreck. She had travelled to her husband's estates and recovered there. Her passage back to England had been thwarted several times by storms and pirates, but she was now looking forward to picking up the threads of the life she had left behind. The account made her sound exciting, adventurous, and slightly dangerous—things a man might struggle to resist.

Helen folded the newspaper and put it on the table, her appetite for breakfast gone. She could not compete with the beautiful Lady Arabella, and now that James was a marquess, he would no doubt want to return to Arabella who would make a much more suitable wife. She was both accomplished and beautiful, not to mention the fact that from what James had told her, Arabella would be able to use her experiences to make her one of the most fascinating women in London society. And once the gossip had died down, she would no doubt want to pick up where she had left off with James.

Her musings were cut short by the arrival of Gillott, just ahead of James. "Beg pardon, Miss Helen, but his lordship would not take no for an answer."

James strode into the room, Helen's heart nearly stopping at the sight of him. The dark blue jacket molded to his broad shoulders and his buckskin trousers clung tightly to his muscular thighs before disappearing into highly polished hessians. His dark hair was messy and looked as though he had spent some time running his hand through it, and her heart sank. He had come to break off their engagement, she knew it.

"It's perfectly fine, Gillott, his lordship and I will take some tea in the small green sitting room, and perhaps you could ask Mrs. Gillott to sit with us."

"Of course, Miss Helen." Gillot departed throwing a disapproving look toward James as he left.

The small green sitting room was one of Helen's favourite rooms in her grandmother's house, and she seated herself on one of the two armchairs by the fire. There was no point in waiting for the axe to fall. She pasted a smile on her face. "I believe I know why you are here, Lord Tremaine."

There was a look of relief on James' face. "You do? Thank God for that." His expression quickly changed to a frown, realizing she had addressed him formally as Lord Tremaine, and the hairs on the back of his neck rose.

She nodded, hoping she could get through the next few moments without the tears falling. All the hurts and cruelty she had suffered at the hands of her aunt and cousin were nothing to the pain she was feeling now. "Of course," she replied calmly, "I understand completely." She stood, readying herself to escort him to the door and cry alone.

James looked puzzled. "Helen, what are you doing?"

"I believe I should feel better doing this standing," she replied.

"Doing what?" James stood in front of her.

She took a breath. "I am releasing you from our engagement so that you may return to your first love." She gripped her skirts and looked at the floor. She could not bear to see the look of relief on his face. "It is a good thing our betrothal was not made fully public. You will need to cancel the notice in *The Times* of course, I will tell my uncle and Grandmama…"

He could not believe his ears. He gently cupped her face in his hands and made her look at him. "I have no idea what you are talking about, sweetheart," he said gently.

"But Lady Arabella…" she began.

"Means nothing to me," he interrupted. "I apologize for my behaviour last night, I should have explained there and then, but I was so shocked to see her that all other thoughts fled me."

"But you love her," she persisted.

"I loved her when I was a boy, Helen, a callow youth who did not know the true meaning of love. I love you, Helen, and you alone, and I will never love another now that I am older and perhaps a little wiser, and I know what I feel for you is so deep I feel it in my soul. Without you, I would be incomplete. You make me whole. I want to spend the rest of my life with you, and I believe I am right in thinking that you feel the same."

She could not look away from his piercing eyes, almost feeling him willing her to believe him. "But…"

"No more buts, darling," he muttered as he silenced her with his lips, touching gently at first then with increasing passion as she leaned into him. He groaned with pleasure as he gathered her into his arms, wanting to feel every inch of her pressed against his body, which had hardened as soon as he touched her. He was almost undone when she opened her lips and gently touched his tongue with her own. He was barely able to stop himself from removing all her clothing and taking her on the rug before the fire. He had to content himself with drawing her onto his lap. "James," she gasped, "what if Gillott, or Mrs. Gillott, or worse, Grandmama should come in?"

"If your grandmother were to come in, I imagine she would not bat an eyelid. Your butler, however, is likely to come after me with a blunderbuss, so I shall restrain myself." He set her beside him but refused to let go of her hand. "When we are married, my sweet, I shall make love to you in every room of every house I own," he promised. "I shall remove all your clothing slowly, piece by piece, until you are naked, and I shall feast my eyes on your body before kissing and caressing every inch of you. Then, when you are ready, I shall ensure that you feel the greatest pleasure you have ever known."

He was suddenly serious, remembering that young women generally went to the marriage bed with little knowledge or understanding of what was to happen. He did not want that for Helen, he wanted her to come to him without fear. He wanted her to want him as much as he wanted her, but she was an intelligent woman and he wanted to be honest with her. He doubted that Lady Eunice had ever taken the trouble to tell her anything. "You do know," he said, gently stroking her shoulder, "that there may be a moment of pain for you." He dropped a kiss on her hair, breathing in the scent of her. "It is momentary, and believe me, if I could avoid it, I would, but there is no other way. After that, I promise it will never hurt again and I know we will be good together."

Helen turned her face to his and kissed his cheek. "I know you would never do anything to hurt me as I would never do anything to hurt you," she said simply.

"Thank God I found you, Miss Nobody," he rasped, taking her lips again.

If he could have kissed her doubt entirely away, he would have done it until the end of time, but he knew he needed to give an explanation for his behaviour last night. Finally, he faced her. "I must apologize for last night. Seeing Arabella like that threw every thought from my head."

"You looked as though you had seen a ghost," she murmured.

"I thought I had, or at least that my mind was playing tricks with me. As far as I knew, as far as anyone knew, Arabella was dead. I even attended a memorial service for her. To see her alive and well was, to say the least, a shock." He grimaced. "But of course, that is probably what Arabella intended. She was always fond of a drama, and what better way to announce her arrival than in front of the audience at the theatre."

Helen smiled wryly. "I cannot imagine that she came straight from the boat dressed for the opera."

James closed his eyes momentarily before drawing some sheets of paper from his pocket. "This arrived early this morning. I had not slept and was about to go out for a ride to clear my head, but I read it and I came straight here." He held the letter out to her. "I want you to read it, Helen. Remember, no secrets between us," he added as she hesitated to take it.

She looked up at him quickly before she took it and began reading.

Dearest James,

I imagine that you were more than a little surprised to see me at the opera last night, given the tale of my demise. However, let me assure you that I am not a ghost or spirit, but alive and well, and more than happy to be back in the heart of society once more.

No doubt you are wondering what happened in the intervening years since we last saw each other. You, I understand from my parents, have done extremely well, not only rich and with a great degree of power and influence in politics, but already a marquess and one day to be a duke. How proud you and your family must be.

My own story is less successful. When we boarded the Florian, *it quickly became apparent that I had made a huge mistake in my ill-advised elopement with Peter. Not only did he drink, which made him short-tempered and at times violent, but I soon learned he had expectations of a fortune from me. He was less than pleased to learn that although I had position and breeding, I had no fortune to speak of. As to his own fortune, let us say that it was greatly exaggerated and perhaps I should have guessed something was amiss by the way he had avoided all contact with his family in London. I was beginning to regret our marriage almost before the* Florian *set sail from Ireland. I was certainly regretting what I had so willfully thrown away with you.*

The crossing was stormy, but when we were blown onto the rocks, the boat quickly broke up. Peter and I were separated, I was one of the lucky ones to be in the lifeboat that was rescued by a passing clipper. When I last saw Peter, he was swimming toward our lifeboat when he was suddenly drawn underneath the water.

When we finally arrived in New York, I went to the home of one of the cousins Peter had told me about. Fortunately, Peter had written about our marriage and our voyage, so I was not too much of a shock. He was kind to me and I believe I could have stayed with him and his family for longer, but I wanted to visit the estate in New Hampshire I had now inherited from Peter. His cousin did try to dissuade me, but you of all people know what I am like when my mind is made up to do something, no matter how harebrained the scheme.

Fortunately, I had sewn some of my jewellery into my clothing to stop Peter from gambling it away with the captain and his crew. I sold some of it to finance the journey to New Hampshire. Having seen some of the elegant buildings in New York, I had hopes that I would be living in a degree of comfort. I was wrong. The large, new house that Peter had lovingly described belonged not to him, but to a neighbouring estate. Peter's house was little more than a log cabin close to the edge of a lake surrounded by forest. There were two servants who seemed determined never to understand a word I said. In winter we were cut off by snow for weeks and in summer there were bears and wolves. I have never been so frightened or alone. The only thing that gave me comfort was thinking of you at home. I knew I had made a terrible mistake and I hope to make it up to you one day. I had thought that Peter was an honourable man, but now I realized that the honourable man was you. I cannot tell you how very much I regret the hurt I caused my parents and friends, but mostly the hurt I caused you, but I digress.

How I survived that first winter, I do not know. In the summer, the money to support the estate is made through lumber, what we would call woodcutting. There is a huge demand for it, but that meant employing men to do the work. I found I had neither the funds nor the authority to do so, even with a manager, and I could not raise enough to make it pay. After three harsh winters and summers terrorized by bears and all kinds of dangerous and unfamiliar creatures, I could take no more. I have been forced by circumstances to work for every bite of food I put in my mouth, for which I do not complain, in fact, not knowing where the next meal is to come from gave me a greater insight into the lives of the poor than distributing baskets of food on my father's estate or even setting up the school for the poor. Had Peter survived and worked the land, I believe we might have made a success, but I knew I could not survive long in that miserable condition and desperately wanted to come home. I left for New York and, with the little money I had left, bought a passage home on the Carolina.

I had no idea that my death had been reported here until I heard the sailors discussing the loss of the Florian. *They did not know who I was as I was travelling under the name of Mrs. Hoyland, as no doubt you know, a woman travelling alone is less open to scandal if she is a respectable widow. I arrived in London a week ago, much to my parents' shock. Sadly, I find them much altered, Father's hair is quite white now and Mother is but a shadow of her former self.*

I have been at my parents' house since arriving home, but now I am ready to enter society again. I must once again ask you to try to forgive my previous behaviour. I was swept away in what I believed to be love only to find it was merely infatuation and worse, the man I thought I loved was not the man neither you nor I thought him to be when you introduced him to me.

I shall always regret leaving with Peter, I did not realize the value of what I had with you until it was too late, and I know this is little consolation for the hurt I caused, but the last few years have been punishment for my wickedness.

I hope you can find it in your heart to forgive a little and that one day we may be friends once again.

Yours, with affection,
Lady Arabella Walmesly

CHAPTER 13

*H*elen folded the sheets and held them out to James. "That is quite a story," she murmured.

"If it can be believed."

Her eyes shot to his. "What do you mean?"

"I have no doubt that Arabella had a difficult time, but she was never one to let the truth get in the way of a good story," he responded wryly. "I have no doubt that she will thoroughly enjoy playing the role of heroic widow. She will find some way to bring this to her advantage. Arabella has always craved attention."

Helen looked at him steadily. "Well, if you have seen the newspapers this morning, you will see that she has it. They are full of her exploits, not in the detail she wrote here, but enough to keep the readers hungry for more."

James laughed. "Indeed, then let us hope that gives her satisfaction. I have no desire to speak of Arabella anymore. Her part in my life is over." Once more, he took her in his arms. "I want to talk about our life together. If we do not marry soon I shall become a suitable candidate for bedlam," he said, pulling his features in what was supposed to make him look like a child pleading for sweetmeats.

Helen laughed. "You do exaggerate, James."

"You think I jest? When we are at a ball, I want to call out all the men who dance with you. I know jealousy is ridiculous, I know I am being ridiculous, but there it is. I want you for myself," he grumbled. "In the unfortunately rare occurrences we are alone, it is even worse. I just want to strip your clothes and make love to you. I want to hear you scream my name. Even when I am alone, you are always in my thoughts and at night you are in my dreams. I will never get enough of you. Say the word and I will get a special license so we can be married by the end of the week."

"That will not do, Tremaine." Neither of them had heard the dowager enter the room and they quickly sprang apart. "Oh, you need not bother on my account, my dears," she said, smiling wickedly. "Now, if you have finished, the pair of you, Gillott has been waiting outside for ten minutes with the tea. "I believe we are a little beyond that, are we not? I do not agree with a special license, it is not the done thing at all, it would cause gossip and may affect Helen's acceptance by society. Now, I think the Newsham Ball is the perfect time for you to be announced as Lady Helen and for your engagement to become public."

"But I am not sure…" Helen began.

"It is perfect," her grandmother ploughed on. "If we were to wait for you, my dear, frankly, you would never be sure. There are times when you must grab the bull by the horns so to speak. Besides, everyone will be there, including Eunice, and I cannot wait to see her face on either count," she cackled. "Now, Gillott, bring in the tea."

Helen could not help but smile as she looked at her fiancé helping her grandmother to tea. Even the powerful Marquess of Woodville knew when he was beaten by the formidable old lady. By the end of the second cup, they had agreed on a wedding date four weeks hence, in the small church in Rockingham where Helen had grown up and where her own parents had been married. The wedding party would be small, James' brother would stand with him, and her grandmother and the Earl and Countess of Rockingham would be invited as her only other living relatives, but she doubted they would come.

They had just finished tea when a letter was brought in for Helen. She glanced at it and pinned a smile on her face. "It's from Mr. Thompson, my publisher, reminding me of our meeting this afternoon," she lied.

"I can come with you," James offered. "Then perhaps we might take a drive in the park."

"Oh, do not go to the trouble on my account." Helen smiled, her heart racing. "I cannot know how long the meeting will be and I do not want to waste your time. I know how busy you are. I am sure Grandmama can spare Lucy to be my chaperone for a few hours."

Her grandmother nodded.

"That's settled then, I shall see you this evening at Lady Harper's musicale."

"You are rather pale, my dear, are you feeling quite well?" her grandmother enquired as James left.

"Just a little tired and I have a slight headache. I think I am a little nervous about meeting Mr. Thompson. He may have changed his mind." Helen had never been one to lie, yet now they seemed to trip off her tongue.

"Nonsense," the dowager scoffed. "He knows a good thing when he sees one. Now go and rest before your meeting, we do not want you looking piqued this evening."

Rest was the last thing Helen wanted, so she dressed carefully in a deep rose gown with a matching pelisse and bonnet, not for her meeting with Mr. Thompson, but for the one that was to follow.

Mr. Thompson was extremely positive about her writing and delighted that she had brought him the first few chapters of her next work. It was a relief when he looked over them and asked when he might have the rest, as she had been worried that her first work might have been a fluke. Mr. Thompson understood that she wanted to remain anonymous. She needed time to get used to the idea of being Lady Helen Rockingham, let alone a Marchioness and someday Duchess. If one day the time was right, she would be happy to be known as an authoress, but for the moment it was an added complication.

She was shocked into silence at the figure Mr. Thompson quoted for her book and even further surprised when, a moment later, he took her silence for disappointment and offered her more. With his words of encouragement still ringing in her ears, she settled into the carriage with added confidence. No matter what was thrown at her in the next meeting, she was now not only a respected writer, she would one day become a woman of substance by her own merit.

When they arrived at their destination, she turned to Lucy and asked her not to tell the dowager about it. "I will not ask you to lie, but if you could avoid the subject, I will be very grateful."

Lucy nodded.

As she entered the opulent sitting room, she heard a voice she was not expecting. Lady Eunice and Lady Clarice were sitting together with

Lady Arabella. None of them rose as she entered. "Ah, here you are at last, Helen, you are late. Now perhaps we may have some tea. Clarice, ring the bell. Helen, do sit down, you are making the place look untidy." Helen sat in the chair facing the others.

"I do not believe you have had the pleasure of meeting Lady Arabella Walmsley," her aunt continued smoothly. "She was betrothed to the Marquess of Woodville some time ago."

Helen somehow managed to smile. Lady Arabella was even more stunning close up than she had been at the opera. Her golden hair was swept up in a loose chignon from which tendrils escaped to frame her delicate face. Clearly the hardships she had described in her letter had left little evidence on her face. She returned Helen's smile but there was little warmth in it.

Her eyes narrowed. "I believe I saw you at the opera in Tremaine's box," she said. Helen nodded. "*The Beggar's Opera*, was it not?" asked Lady Arabella.

There was complete silence while the maid brought in tea and set it on the small walnut table near her aunt's chair. "Hardly something suitable for a young woman to see." Her aunt sniffed. "That is what comes of you being in your grandmother's care. I am rapidly coming to the opinion that both you and your grandmother need to be taken care of to protect the family's reputation."

Helen's head shot up. "I was well-chaperoned, my lady, by one of your dear friends. Lord Tremaine's mother was in attendance."

"I am beginning to think that Lady Tremaine is less of a friend than I thought," her aunt muttered.

Arabella delicately replaced her cup and saucer on the table. "Tell me, Miss Rockingham, what is the nature of your relationship with Lord Woodville?" Helen sat up straight. She had thought Arabella wanted James back since she had read the letter, but it was now clear that she was right. With James possessing both money and a title, Arabella was ready to stake a claim on him once more. Helen looked her in the eye. "Whether I have a relationship with Lord Tremaine or whether I do not is really none of your concern, my lady."

"Really, Helen, remember who you are, that is no way to speak to your betters," the countess snapped.

Arabella smiled. "Do not trouble yourself on my behalf, Lady Eunice. I am quite sure that Miss Rockingham and I understand each other, or at least we shall by the time she leaves here." Her voice was smooth, but there was a hint of malice as she emphasized Helen's lack of title which Helen did not bother to correct. "As you know, Tremaine and I have known each other since we were both in leading strings. James was wildly in love with me and we were to have married in a match that had the blessing of both our families."

"But you abandoned him at the altar and married someone else," Helen interrupted, her temper rising.

Arabella took a breath before continuing smoothly, "Rather ancient history now, but it is true I married and went to America to start a new life. I am sure you have read my story in the newspapers." Helen nodded.

Arabella smiled again. "It seems I have become something of a *cause celebre*. The newspapers are commissioning my portrait and as everyone wants to know my story, I have been invited to every grand function in London, including those at Carlton House. Even the Prince Regent himself is fascinated," she said, eyeing Lady Eunice to see the affect her words were having.

"But you broke his heart," Helen blurted out. "You broke his heart and humiliated him."

Arabella turned her piercing eyes back to Helen. "He recovered. In fact, it was probably the thing he needed. Following our broken engagement, he began to take life seriously. It made him go and make sufficient money to support a wife and family, and correct me if I am wrong, but was it not his newfound drive and ambition that brought him to the attention of the Duke of Bainbridge who made him heir? In a way, one might say that I was the making of him."

"Of course," Lady Eunice agreed. "Men often need a nudge to bring them up to snuff."

Helen returned Arabella's gaze. "And now you want to take up where you left off."

Arabella tilted her head to one side. "You are not as green as I was led to believe, Miss Rockingham."

"And you believe that I must be some sort of threat to your plan, which is why I am here."

"She stole him from me," Clarice put in sulkily. "He was about to make an offer and she took him."

Arabella ignored the interruption. "James Tremaine is mine. I let him go once and I am not about to do it again." The blue eyes flashed, and her lips thinned. She suddenly looked older and the famous beauty had disappeared.

"But he no longer loves you."

"He loved me once, I can make him love me again."

Helen could only feel sympathy. All of Arabella's future was tied up in her past. Time had moved on, James had moved on, but she would be wise not to antagonize her opponent. Arabella was a survivor and would fight to the death to get what she wanted. "I feel sorry for you, my lady, but you cannot make a person love you," she said, glancing at her aunt. "Believe me, I know. Now, please excuse me," she said and rose. "I have been gone all afternoon and Grandmama will wonder where I am."

As she approached the door, it opened, and the butler intoned, "Lord James Tremaine."

---

*J*ames had only to take one look at Helen's face to see that the meeting had not been a pleasant one. He bowed to the women as though his dropping in on them was a regular occurrence. He could explain his sudden appearance to Helen later. He took her arm, guided her to her chair and she sank down. He moved a chair to sit next to her and as he was sitting, managed to briefly brush his fingers against hers. "Ladies," he greeted them. "How fortunate to have caught all of you together. I am having a small celebratory dinner next week and I should be delighted if you would do me the honour of attending," he improvised. Arabella was definitely a surprise, but he could hardly leave her out of the invitation.

"We shall be delighted, my lord," the countess gushed.

"A celebration, how exciting, what are you celebrating, Tremaine?" Arabella's voice cut in.

For the first time since she had left him, James turned and looked at Arabella. She was still beautiful, he could not deny it, but for the first time he noticed the hardness in her eyes and the set of her mouth. Had it always been there, or had he only just opened his eyes to her? There was even an edge to her voice and he began to wonder if he ever truly knew her at all. "Ah, it is to be a surprise, all will be revealed on the evening." He looked forward to seeing their surprise when he revealed his betrothal to Helen.

"I do hope that you and your grandmother will come, Miss

Rockingham," he said as he turned to Helen with a gleam in his eyes. He knew this would enrage the countess, and he was not disappointed.

"Oh, I doubt that Helen will be able to come. She does not often go into society and has recently been unwell. Rich food and too much excitement are not good for her nervous condition," Lady Eunice was quick to reply.

"I am sorry to hear that you have been ill, Miss Rockingham, are you recovered?" he asked in a tone that, to Helen, was clear he did not believe a word her aunt said. Whether her aunt heard it, she could not tell, but returning his grin, she replied, "I am quite recovered now, thank you, Lord Tremaine."

"Then I must insist that you attend."

"If you insist, sir, then I shall be delighted to attend," she replied as innocently as she could.

"I am at a loss to understand what you might be celebrating, Tremaine. It is not your birthday, could it perhaps be a successful trading deal, or is it that one of your ships has returned bearing a precious cargo?" Arabella smiled.

"As I said, Lady Walmesly, all will be revealed on the evening."

Arabella frowned. "Come, Tremaine, you have been calling me by my first name for years, and we have shared many memories, surely there is no need to be so formal."

He inclined his head. "As you say, Lady Walmesly, many memories and not all of them pleasant."

There was a sharp intake of breath as the other women took in the cutting remark. "It was a long time ago, Tremaine," Arabella said softly.

"As you say, a long time ago, and I think we are both older and wiser," he said evenly. "Now..." He rose. "I believe you were leaving when I arrived, Miss Rockingham, may I offer you a ride?"

"Wait a moment, Helen." They had almost forgotten that Clarice was present until she jumped up. "I found this, you must have left it behind when you were sent to Yorkshire." She held out a parcel wrapped in brown paper and tied with string. "It's just some of your scribblings, I was going to put them on the fire, but now you are here you might as well have them. She fancies herself a writer," she explained to Arabella, laughing.

James turned back. "I take it that you do not know that Miss Rockingham is to be a published author."

"That is just fanciful nonsense," Lady Eunice retorted. "Helen makes up stories because she is a wicked, deceitful, and ungrateful girl, and I apologize if she has misled you, my lord. Believe me, no one will publish her work, and if they did, no one would have the slightest interest in reading it."

Before James could draw breath to reply, Helen said firmly, "We shall have to see, Aunt, we shall have to see." She swept from the room.

"*I* sent your grandmother's carriage home," James explained as he handed her in. "Your maid as well, though as far as the harpies in there know, she is already ensconced in the carriage performing her chaperone duties. What were you thinking, going to see those three?"

"Well, in the first place, I was summoned by my aunt and in the second place, I had no idea Lady Arabella would be there. I did not know my aunt knew her. But more to the point, how did you come to both know where I was and drop in to visit?" She looked at him suspiciously.

James leaned back against the velvet squabs. "Your grandmother discovered the note, it must have fallen from your pocket, and she sent word to say you had gone to the lions' den, or should I say the lioness' den?"

"More like a pit of vipers," Helen replied crisply.

He laughed. "I recall the first time we met, you reminded me that in the jungle, the lionesses do the hunting."

"And they work together to isolate and pick off their quarry."

James frowned. "I am not sure now who is the quarry, you or me."

Helen thought for a moment. "Both, I think."

His eyes narrowed. "What did Arabella want?"

"I think she wanted to give me a warning."

"What sort of a warning?"

Helen laughed. "Honestly, James, how can you be so obtuse? Lady Arabella is back and intends to marry you. Indeed, she takes some credit that her elopement was the making of you."

"She what?" James exclaimed.

"She believes that her leaving spurred you on to become powerful and rich and led to you becoming heir to the Duke of Bainbridge. Without the anger she caused, you would still be a poor second son. I believe that having been the cause of your success, Lady Arabella intends to ensure that she wears the duchess's coronet. I am not sure," she added, "whether you are to have much of a say in the matter."

James' eyebrows very nearly disappeared into his hair. "Surely, after all these years and everything she has done, she cannot believe that she can just pick up where she left off."

"I believe she does, in fact, her words were, 'He loved me once, I can make him love me again.'"

His mouth set in a thin line. "Arabella does not know the meaning of the word 'love,' all she understands is money and position. Whoever she eventually marries, she will never love the man. All she will love are the gowns and jewels he will give her, and the status his position will bring. She will no doubt produce the all-important heir as fair trade and then spend the rest of her days making his life a misery until he seeks comfort in the arms of a mistress—who she will blame—without thinking for one moment that she has caused her own unhappiness and that of all around her."

Helen paused for a moment before replying, "I believe you are right."

James crushed her to him, kissing her deeply, then drew back slightly to brush an errant curl from her cheek. "That is not the sort of marriage we will have, my love. You and I will wake up together, we will raise our children together, talk together, and when we have disagreements, which I am sure at times we will, we will work things out together."

Helen leaned in so that their foreheads touched. "Does this mean that you will not take a mistress?" From whispered conversations in the dormitory at school, she recalled that some of the girls knew their fathers kept mistresses, indeed, some of them knew that their fathers had other families elsewhere.

James smiled at her. "I shall have no need of a mistress since you will be both my day life and my night life. Something that I intend will bring us both a great deal of pleasure."

Helen sighed dramatically. "And what of the jewels and gowns, am I not to be covered in them?" She grinned.

"Oh, you shall have gowns, some for the public to see and some just for my pleasure." He smiled wickedly. "As for jewels, I intend to cover you from head to toe in diamonds, sapphires, rubies, and emeralds and anything else your heart desires. Sometimes my heart will desire that all you are wearing will be jewels, no gown,"—he kissed her temple—"no stays,"—he kissed her ear—"absolutely nothing but jewels." He took her mouth in a heart-stopping kiss.

Helen drew back. "Actually, what I should really appreciate more than anything is a good supply of paper, pens, and ink. Aunt Eunice made me feel as though I was asking for diamond-encrusted quills when I asked and gave me little sparingly."

James could not help but laugh. "Here I am throwing my wealth at your feet and all you want are writing materials."

Helen thought for a moment. "I suppose you are vastly wealthy, I mean, I should have thought of it before, of course."

James shook his head. "Helen, you are priceless. I imagine you are the only woman in London who does not know down to the last penny how much money I have. But let me set your mind at rest. After I have showered you in jewels, there will still be money left for as many writing materials as you want."

Helen's eyes darkened. "I do not need jewels or fine gowns, James. I have never had them and do not need them, honestly."

"I know, my love, perhaps it is that I need to give them to you."

"But you have given me so much already."

He placed a finger on her lips. "No, my sweet, you have given me something I never thought I would have. You have given me your love and mended my heart. I thought I would never love again until I met you. You, my darling, are my own precious jewel."

CHAPTER 14

*A*s soon as she and her grandmother were announced, Helen knew something was wrong. The eyes of all of London's finest society followed them, the chatter of three hundred well-bred voices stilled as they approached, small groups moved away as they passed, and some turned their backs as they drew near. She had expected a degree of curiosity, but the mood was chilly if not downright hostile.

"Straighten your shoulders and smile," her grandmother said quietly. "I do not know what has gone on here, but believe me, I fully intend to find out."

As she passed, Helen could not help but hear some of the whispered comments.

"Her mother's family were miners."

"I heard she was born out of wedlock."

"Scandalous."

"She's no more a lady than the barbary ape at the royal menagerie."

"Eunice must be spitting feathers," one old dowager cackled.

"Pretty enough, but no breeding of course."

"I heard she has already borne a child. Like mother like daughter, and not a wedding band between them. Disgraceful conduct and disgraceful that she should come here."

"Poor Lady Tremaine, one son married to an unsuitable bride, but two?"

"Of course the Newshams had no idea of her low birth when they extended the invitation."

"I thought she was some kind of paid companion to Lady Clarice. I believe the old woman has finally gone gaga, adopting her as her granddaughter."

It was a relief when they reached the comparative seclusion of an alcove, as Helen's face could grow no whiter. "Sit down and take deep breaths, my dear," her grandmother said quietly, not quite masking the anger Helen could hear in it. "This is Eunice's work, I will be bound. I must apologize, Helen, I seriously underestimated the lengths she would go to in order to punish you."

"But why does Lady Eunice want to punish me? What have I done?"

The dowager was interrupted by the arrival of Lady Tremaine, a man who looked almost exactly like James, and a young woman dressed in a stunning gown of emerald green who said, "You must be the lovely Helen James has told us about. I am Emily Tremaine, his sister-in-law. I feel sure we shall be great friends." As she spoke, Emily reached out to touch her arm reassuringly. "Do not concern yourself about the ridiculous things that are being said, dear. James will be here soon, and all will be well, I promise you. In the meantime, this is my husband, Robert Tremaine, who would be delighted to dance with you."

Helen curtseyed to both. "I am not sure," she murmured as she anxiously bit her lip.

"Oh, these people will have forgotten everything by the time supper is served. Some of them have dogs who are more intelligent than their owners. Besides, you will shortly have some of the most powerful men in the country at hand, and the nobility know which side their bread is buttered on, believe me."

She paused for a moment before adding, "If it is any consolation, before we were married, my husband thought I had stolen the diamonds I am wearing tonight, so if I can live that down, I believe by the end of the ball you will have the cream of London society eating out of the palm of your hand." She patted the diamond necklace. "I see you know something of this tale. Arabella took them and spread it about that I had stolen them because at the time she fancied herself in love with my husband before she got her claws into James. It's a long tale and I shall tell it to you one day."

The Duke of Witney held out his hand. "Enough chat for now,

Emily. If I am not dancing with Helen before James arrives, he will have my guts for garters." He turned to Helen. "Shall we?"

As they danced, Robert regaled her with stories of his childhood with James. She was still laughing at the prospect of James hanging from an oak tree by his trousers when they had fallen out of a tree house they had built when the music came to a stop. All around them, people stopped dancing, the women sunk into deep curtseys, and the men bowed. The groups parted and as Helen became aware of not only James, but the man beside him walking toward them, she hastily sank down in a curtsey.

She was shocked when a white-gloved hand appeared in front of her face. "Allow me, my dear." She was being helped up by none other than the Prince Regent himself. "You must be the beautiful Helen James has been telling me about. Although,"—he turned to James—"you did not do justice to her beauty. This Helen would rival she of Troy, I am sure. In fact, I shall insist that the next ship the navy builds shall be called the *Lady Helen*. Would you do me the honour of a dance?" he asked graciously.

Before she knew what was happening, she was swept onto the dance floor. "I understand you have been having a little family trouble, my dear." The prince smiled down at her. "Believe me, it happens in the best of families."

"For some reason, everyone here seems to think I am both the daughter of a fallen woman and a fallen woman myself, which is entirely too many fallen women for one evening," she ventured, then stammered, "I am so sorry, Your Highness, I should not have said that."

The prince laughed. "My dear, if we are keeping a tally of fallen women, my illustrious ancestor Charles the Second would win on his own." He glanced round before whispering, "Though there are some here who would come a close second. Your grandfather was a mining engineer, yes? I believe men of industry, science, and business are the ones who will lead the way in future. Never be ashamed of your past."

"I am not, Your Highness," she replied boldly. "I believe men should be respected for what they achieve in their lives…"—she paused for a moment—"and women."

The prince raised an eyebrow. "My, I wonder if Tremaine realizes that he is introducing another radical into his family. Robert has his hands full with dear Emily, but I rather suspect you may be even more of a challenge. James tells me you are about to publish a novel."

Helen nodded.

"I should like to read it, and should you wish to dedicate it to me, I shall be most happy for you to do so. I, for one, think it is time that women should have more control over their lives." He smiled. "As should princes," he added.

Her head shot up. "But surely, Sir, as the Prince of Wales, you can do as you please."

"Ah, unfortunately, sending people to the Tower and chopping heads off has been out of fashion for some time." He grinned.

She smiled back. "I was not thinking of anything quite so extreme, though I wager there are times when you wish you could."

He threw back his head and laughed. "Just tell me which of these harridans has been annoying you and I will see what I can do."

"Perhaps Lady Alton over there, she should spend some time in the Tower for the crime of wearing rather too many dead birds and pieces of fruit in her hair," Helen suggested.

"Perhaps the birds were attracted by the fruit and died after becoming entangled in that rather vulgar wig," he suggested.

"Or Sir Peter Hadsell who needs to be locked in a darkened room for inflicting that orange waistcoat on his lilac pantaloons."

"A heinous crime," he agreed, "and perhaps a few minutes on the rack so that he does not need to totter about on the high heels he seems to think none of us notice."

Helen lowered her voice. "Perhaps you should suggest a new law concerning crimes of fashion," she suggested.

"I rather think I might. I must say I have enjoyed our dance enormously, Lady Helen. However, now I fear I must return you to Tremaine before he stamps over here and calls me out, though I should like it if you and Tremaine would dine with me at Carlton House soon."

"I am sure I should be honoured, Your Highness."

By the time they returned to where James and his family were standing, the atmosphere in the room had completely changed. Instead of the sharp looks and pointed glances directed at her, people were smiling and waving in greeting.

"London society is still as fickle as it ever was," James commented, tucking her hand firmly through his arm.

"I cannot believe that I just danced with the prince," Helen murmured.

"You not only danced with him, he was enjoying it. What caused you both so much hilarity?"

"His Royal Highness and I have decided that there should be a law passed regarding crimes of fashion, and we were deciding who our first victims should be." She laughed.

"I knew you would charm him, as you charm everyone you meet." He smiled down at her.

Finally, now that Helen relaxed, James could do the same. "Come with me, there is someone I want you to meet."

"Who am I going to meet?" Helen asked curiously. "After the Prince of Wales, I cannot imagine who you are going to spring on me."

James grinned. "Prinny was eaten up with curiosity, he was happy to meet you. When my mother and brother arrived, they were instantly aware of the vicious rumours being spread and sent word to me. As it happens, I was at the palace. His Royal Highness was happy to come to the aid of a damsel in distress, but the person I am about to introduce you to will have a far more personal influence on our lives," he said as he pushed open the oak door.

The salon was decorated in the latest style, the walls were hung with pale green silk with darker velvet drapes at the three sets of windows. Several sofas and chairs were scattered throughout the room and a grand piano stood at one end. A cheerful fire burned in the grate before which were several armchairs. As they came further into the room, a man slowly stood from his warm seat by the fire.

"Ah, so this is the lovely Lady Helen Rockingham." His voice was soft with age.

"Helen, may I present His Grace, the Duke of Bainbridge," James said.

Helen sank into a deep curtsey. "It is a pleasure to meet you, Your Grace."

"Come closer, my dear, and sit by me. I am afraid neither my eyes nor my knees are what they once were. Now," he went on, as she settled herself on the sofa, "tell me about yourself. You are Jonathon's child I believe, a sad business." He shook his head. "Your grandfather was a good man, but stubborn to the point of stupidity at times."

"Did you know him, Sir?" Helen asked.

"We were at school together." He smiled. "The pool of rank is both narrow and shallow. Your grandfather was always in trouble. If there was a rule, Thomas thought it was his duty to break it. Sadly, he inherited his title much too young and the responsibilities of the dukedom weighed heavily upon him. His father had been somewhat profligate, and Thomas had the Devil's own job keeping the estate together. By the time he had his own family, he had turned into a humourless, some would say *tyrant*. He would brook no opposition and that led to problems when it came to your father's match I believe, partly because Jonathon was as headstrong as his father and refused the bride his father had chosen. But this is all old news. Tell me something of yourself."

The old man listened carefully as Helen spoke. "And in your uncle's house, you were raised properly and not mistreated?"

"My uncle has been kind."

"And your aunt?"

The old man's eyes were faded, but Helen was aware of both the perception and intelligence behind them. She did not want to speak ill of the woman, but neither was she prepared to lie. "My aunt did her Christian duty, Sir."

He regarded her steadily before commenting, "Which I imagine was not much. Eunice has had many disappointments in her life and I imagine being made to take you in was a constant reminder of the greatest one."

Helen frowned. "I do not follow, Your Grace."

The duke smiled. "It is not for me to tell. Now, tell me about this book Tremaine says you are to have published—a woman being published could never have happened in my day. Times are certainly changing, and I believe for the better."

The next hour passed quickly and they talked and laughed until the old man rose. "Forgive me, my dears, but I must take my leave." He turned to James. "You have chosen well. Helen will make an excellent Marchioness, and in a few months, a wonderful duchess."

"Oh, no, Your Grace, surely it will be years before…" Helen began.

The duke held up his hand. "I do not believe in varnishing the truth, my dear, my doctors here in town have told me that my heart is failing. In fact, that I am still here at all seems quite a mystery to them." He chuckled. "However, I shall not last much longer, and when I die, I do not want you to mourn. I have had a long and happy life, that is what you must celebrate. I should like to live long enough to see you married, but if I do not, there is to be no excessive weeping and wailing and wearing of black, all of which I detest. This is all in my will. You will carry on with your plans. Life will go on."

"But I have only just met you, I do not want you to die before I have a chance to get to know you," Helen said quietly.

He clasped her hand. "Then I shall endeavour to confound the physicians further. Now," he turned to James, "ring for my valet. As our hosts know that I am in here chaperoning you, I imagine you might manage a few moments of privacy before you must return to the eyes and wagging tongues of the ton. You see, I am not so old that I do not recall my youth."

As the duke left the room, James locked the door behind him and pocketed the key.

"What are you doing?" Helen asked, startled.

"Ensuring that we are not disturbed, my love," he said and, with a grin, stalked toward her. "I have been patient all evening while you have danced with other men and listened while you have spoken to them, and now I want you in my arms. I want to feel your body on mine."

Helen stepped back. "I would remind you, my lord, that of the two men I danced with, one was your brother and the other was the Prince of Wales, both of whom you set up to dance with me."

"Nevertheless," he said, continuing his advancement, "I find that where you are concerned, I do not care to have any hands on you other than my own."

Helen let out a squeak as her back touched the wall. "What do you plan to do?" she whispered.

"This," he growled as he caught both her hands in his large one. He pulled them over her head and out of the way so he could press his lean, hard body against her as he lowered his head to take her lips in a powerful kiss, his tongue demanding entry to her mouth. Helen could not resist, nor did she want to, and when she touched her tongue to his, he groaned and hauled her into his arms. "It's not enough," he rasped.

His hands roamed over her back while her own hands grasped the front of his jacket, pulling him closer. Her breasts felt swollen with need and her nipples tightened as he gently stroked a hand across them. Her stomach clenched as his hand drifted lower. He began to slide up her skirts and her head fell back as he stroked her thigh. "That's right, my love," he whispered when she moaned softly as he found her most intimate place. "Give yourself to me," he breathed as the pads of his fingers parted her folds and sought the place he knew would send her over the edge. "Let me pleasure you," he said softly as he slipped his fingers into her body.

"Oh, James," she breathed, her mind narrowing as she felt her whole body attune itself solely to the movement of his hand on her breast and his fingers within her.

"That is it, Helen, come for me," he groaned, hearing his own voice thicken with passion, feeling every cell in his body wanting nothing more than to plunge into her again and again and give them both release. But at this moment even more, he wanted to watch her face as she reached her first climax for him.

"Oh my God, James!" He felt her tense as spasm after spasm rocked her deepest core until she collapsed against him. He was as hard as rock, but he would control himself. However, if they did not marry soon, he would be a suitable candidate for bedlam. He could not wait much longer to introduce Helen to the pleasures of making love and she would be a quick and passionate study, of that he was sure.

"I think I may have just died of pleasure," she whispered into the front of his shirt, her voice still a little breathless.

"When we are married, my sweet, I plan to do this and more, much, much more to your delectable body on a daily basis."

Helen raised her head. "But what about you, James? I cannot imagine that the pleasure is just for the benefit of the woman."

He smiled. "Direct as always." He breathed deeply, feeling uncomfortable for the first time. "For a man, the greatest pleasure comes when he is…inside a woman…as my fingers gave you pleasure just now, my…" He searched for the word.

"Appendage? Manhood?" Helen suggested, helpfully.

"All right." He had been going to say "cock," but it did not seem suited to the drawing room. "My manhood will replace my fingers and it will feel so very good for both of us."

"Should we not try it now? It seems unfair that I should experience such bliss without you," Helen asked innocently, her care for him nearly breaking his resolve.

"No, my love, not now," he replied hastily. "For although there is nothing I would rather do than remove every item of clothing and make love to you all night, I will not have a tumble with you at a ball like the worst kind of rake. I will wait," he added grimly, "even if it kills me."

"Very well." Helen tilted her head to one side. "In that case, I think perhaps we should return to the ball, but I must tell you, my lord," she teased, "that I fully intend to hold you to your promise."

CHAPTER 15

There were only two women in the retiring room as Helen entered. "You may go," Lady Arabella ordered her maid, who quickly bobbed a curtsey and left. "So," she addressed Helen through the mirror. "I see you have had an assignation with Tremaine, judging by the state of your clothing and coiffeur, he could never resist running his fingers through hair."

Helen took a deep breath and kept her expression neutral as she approached the dressing table. "I merely came to freshen up, your ladyship, the ballroom is hot and…"

"Oh, please, spare me that nonsense." Arabella sniffed. "You went into the library with Tremaine to meet with the old duke who left several minutes before you. It therefore follows that you and Tremaine were alone together and if I know anything about it, Tremaine will have made the most of the opportunity."

"Your ladyship seems to be remarkably well-informed," Helen replied.

Arabella smiled. "It pays one to be well-informed and one pays to ensure one is."

Determined not to allow herself to appear intimidated, Helen sat on the rose-coloured velvet stool next to Arabella and began to release her hair from its pins. Without a maid to assist, she would have to repair the damage herself.

Lady Arabella watched her for a moment before speaking, "He will not marry you, I hope you know that. I imagine he's already kissed you and touched you, he may even have bedded you—Tremaine is no monk —but as for marriage, when he does marry, it will be to one of his own class."

Helen concentrated on ensuring that her hands were not shaking as she drew the brush through her hair. "You seem extremely sure of yourself, my lady."

Arabella smiled. "Among those of us of rank, marriage is a contract. A man provides financial security and position, a woman provides breeding and a dowry, and as you have neither, Miss Rockingham, it stands to reason that Tremaine, although happy to bed you, will never wed you."

"I would remind you that I am the granddaughter of an earl."

"And I would remind you that you are the daughter of a disinherited son of an earl who coupled with a miner's daughter. You will never be worthy of him."

"Perhaps James does not care about such things," Helen shot back.

Arabella's eyes narrowed. "Perhaps not now, for men's minds are easily led by what lies between their legs but let us suppose for a moment that Tremaine did marry you. Eventually, he would come to resent you when you were not received by the highest families and were only tolerated by the lower ones. All the power and prestige he has worked so hard for would come to naught."

"I do not believe that someone who has repeatedly gained accolades for his work for the government and the prince would so easily lose his position because of his marriage to me," Helen replied, her voice shaking slightly.

Lady Arabella shook her head. "That just shows what a goose you are. With you at his side, he would quickly lose influence and as for the prince, he is notorious for dropping his favourites like the proverbial hotcakes. For the moment, the prince may be fond of Tremaine and taken with you, but fashions change quickly."

To her surprise, Arabella suddenly rose and stood behind her, taking the brush and deftly twisting her hair into a perfect chignon. "I know you fancy yourself in love with him, and I am not unsympathetic," she said softly as she began replacing the jewelled pins. "And if that is the case, ask yourself this—could you live with yourself knowing that if you married him, you had in effect made him less than he is worth?

Tremaine has the talent and ability to become one of the great leaders of our time. Are you willing to deprive him and our nation of that? There." She pushed the last pin into place, scooped up her fan and shawl, and headed to the door.

She paused, her hand on the handle. "If you really love him, you must let him go. Let him live the life he truly deserves."

Helen looked at her own reflection without seeing, her mind tumbling once again. Was Arabella right? Would marriage to her make him a pariah to his peers? James had said that he cared not a fig for the opinions of society, but what if that was not entirely true? He was a proud man, he gained satisfaction from his work and service to his country. If that avenue were to be cut off, would he eventually come to blame and resent her? Arabella clearly wanted him back, she had made no secret of the fact when they had met at her aunt's, and Helen could see that Arabella would make both a perfect duchess and society hostess. She had been raised for it all her life, where Helen had effectively been raised at best to be a governess or companion. Even were she to take her place as Lady Rockingham, her background and upbringing would be always a detriment to her and never forgotten by society. Being the centre of attention was as natural as sunshine to Arabella, whereas Helen had been trained to keep in the shadows.

It did not seem to matter how much James had reassured her that she was the wife he wanted, his voice was drowned out in her mind by Arabella's parting words.

If she really loved him, ought she to let him go and let him live the life he truly deserves?

CHAPTER 16

"*Y*ou look lovely, my dear."

The dowager's words broke into Helen's reverie. "But perhaps I should remind you that you are about to attend your betrothal dinner, not a public execution."

Helen looked down at her dress. The modiste had worked her magic. It was the sheerest pale blue silk with pansies embroidered at the waist and the hem. Everything about it emphasized her features, the colour brought out the colour of her eyes, and the cut of the gown her narrow waist. Lucy had twisted her hair into a simple chignon from which a few tendrils had been teased to frame her face. "I am just a little nervous, that is all," she explained, but in truth she felt sick from Arabella's words going constantly round her mind ever since the ball. If marrying James did in some way decrease his position, could she bear it? He loved her now, of that there was no doubt, but in a few years would he come to hate her and blame her for his falling? She could not bear the thought. He had said that he cared nothing for the opinions of others of his class, but he had always been one of them in truth, she had not. From her position on the sidelines of society, she had firsthand knowledge of how they closed ranks against those whom they considered unacceptable, and once lost, it was almost impossible to gain re-entry, no matter how wealthy or titled. There were some transgressions that were considered completely beyond the pale and marrying someone who was not of the nobility, or was not brought up as such, was one of them.

The thoughts kept her so preoccupied that she was surprised when the coach reached Bainbridge House. "Come along, Helen," her grandmother said, once more bringing her back to the present. "I imagine that Eunice has worked out by now the reason for this evening, though I must confess I am dying to see her face when Tremaine makes the official announcement. I believe he persuaded William to keep it a secret until tonight and that the morning papers will carry the announcement."

Helen could not help but admire the hall with its tasteful cream and gold decor and classical Greek columns topped by gilt-covered leaves supporting a ceiling of delicate fan pattern with the tracings picked out in gold. It was another reminder of the wealth and power of the family to which she would soon belong. As she entered the green salon, she tried to keep her face impassive while she took in the scale of the place. A grand pianoforte stood at one end, yet there was still room for the plentiful sofas and chairs scattered about, and a large chandelier glittered and sparkled in the centre of the room framed by two smaller ones at either end, making it feel light and airy. Despite her impression that the dinner was to be fairly small and intimate between the two families, James had obviously had other ideas. Guests stood in small groups, yet still filled much of the room. She recognized the Duke and Duchess of Whitney and Lady Tremaine, as well as the Duke of Bainbridge, and there were at least two earls and a lord. Standing by one of the large windows, she was dismayed to see, was Lady Arabella and her parents. Lady Arabella laughed at something one of the men near her said.

"I was beginning to wonder where you were." James was all at once by her side, raising her hand to his lips.

"This is rather a larger event than I was expecting," she murmured, as he led her toward his family.

"I could not resist showing you off, and you look spectacular in that gown. Besides," he added, "many of the people here will be only too happy to ensure that you are well-received. Everyone here wants you to take the ton by storm."

"I am not entirely sure that is true of quite all your guests." She nodded toward Arabella, who smiled and raised her champagne glass in what Helen knew could only be an ironic salute."

James' eyes narrowed. "Arabella is here for one reason and one reason only," he said firmly.

"And that is?"

"I want her to know, once and for all, that anything she thought was between us was over a long time ago, that there is no chance of rekindling it, and that you and I are to be married, not to form a dynasty or a political alliance or merely to beget an heir, but because we love each other and want to spend the rest of our lives together. Though," he added with a lecherous wink, "I am sure we shall both greatly enjoy the begetting of an heir."

Helen quirked an eyebrow. "And will you tell her ladyship this, or shall I?"

James grinned. "If necessary, I shall put it in *The Times* along with our betrothal announcement. Though possibly not the part about the begetting of an heir." He laughed.

When they were called to take their places for dinner, her grandmother was escorted by the Duke of Bainbridge and she and James followed. Out of the corner of her eye, she noticed her aunt's look of fury that for once, Helen took precedence. "Does my aunt know the reason for this dinner?" she whispered.

James shook his head. "I doubt it. I made it clear to your uncle that he was to keep our betrothal a secret until I announced it. He seemed pleased enough to do so."

"I doubt the pleasure will last when she gets him home," Helen remarked drily.

"I also," he added thoughtfully, "declined to reveal your title, as you requested."

"Thank you. I know you think I am being a goose about this, but everything I thought I knew about myself has changed and I just need a little more time to get used to the idea of being a Lady."

"You will not have long to get used to one title before you have to get used to another. Very soon you will be a marchioness, and the sooner the better."

The dining room was fit for a royal banquet, set with elegant silverware that gleamed against the snowy-white damask tablecloth while rows of cut glass crystal sparkled from the light of chandeliers and candelabras. White lilies and roses decorated the table and let forth a heady scent. "You must tell me what you think of my chef, my dear," the old duke said as patted her hand. "He produces food to make the angels weep, or so he tells me." He winked, trying to put her at ease, and she smiled back as she took her seat beside him.

Helen looked up and down the richly set table thinking of the meager meals of her childhood and the joyless repasts at her second home. "I shall look forward to the experience, as I have never eaten the food of angels before."

"Well, he is a genius," the duke said and chuckled, "again, so he tells me."

The food was indeed exquisite. Dish after dish arrived, from chestnut soup, salmon with fennel and mint, leg of mutton with oysters, and duck a la mode, a variety of creams and jellies with the transparent pudding with silver web as the grand finale to the meal. Delicious as it all looked, Helen could only manage a few bites, her nervousness increasing with every dish.

Finally, the duke gently tapped his glass. "Dear family and friends, as you know, this is an evening of celebration. I am delighted to announce that my heir, James Tremaine, Marquess of Woodville, is now betrothed to the lovely Miss Helen Rockingham. I would ask that you raise your glasses in a toast and wish them happy." He turned to Helen. "I for one, my dear, could not be happier for you and Tremaine. I know you will not only make a marvellous duchess one day, but you will make him happy."

Helen smiled back. "Thank you, Your Grace."

He turned to James. "And you will ensure that you make this lovely young woman the happiest of brides, or you will answer to me," he said in mock severity.

"I can assure Your Grace that I intend to spend the rest of my life doing precisely that," James said, putting his arm around Helen's waist.

"And get to work on producing an heir. I want to see one before I die," the old duke barked and then chuckled at the shock on Helen's face.

"I shall give it my utmost attention, Your Grace," James said and laughed.

---

*A*fter dinner, the ladies left the men to their port and cigars. Helen was horrified to see that by the time she had accepted the congratulations of some of the ladies, the only seat left in the small blue salon was next to her aunt. "Come, my dear, let me congratulate you," she said as she patted the seat beside her. "The news of your engagement is something of a surprise," she added, "as apparently my husband was sworn to secrecy, but of course you know that, I am sure."

"I wanted some time to get used to the idea," Helen replied honestly.

"Of course, now that your life is about to change, you must accustom yourself to the fact that people will scrutinize your every move. Someone like Lady Arabella, or indeed Clarice, has, of course been raised for such a role, whereas you have always been happy to merge into the background." Her aunt's smile may have looked genuine to someone across the room, but Helen knew better.

Helen was used to shrinking before her aunt, but she lifted her chin. "I was always made to merge into the background, but I am sure that with James' and the Tremaine family's help, I shall be able to rise to the challenge."

"I am sure you will certainly try, and"—Eunice smirked, looking at the young marchioness-to-be—"it is not the first time the family will have attempted to make a silk purse from a sow's ear. I underestimated your ambition, my dear. I quite see now that you were determined to trap Tremaine from the first time you met," she said with narrowed eyes.

Helen's eyes widened. "You thought I schemed to win James?"

"Of course you did," the older woman scoffed. "You were not the first and you will not be the last, especially when a duchess's coronet is at stake. You played your cards very well, poor Clarice never stood a chance. Still," she added, "her engagement to the Earl of Prescot is to be announced the day after yours, and as he is rich and already has an heir, Clarice will not have to be bothered with that side of things," she said distastefully. "All she will be required to do is run his many homes and be a decorative presence."

"The Earl of Prescot? But is he not one of Uncle's friends?"

The countess shrugged. "What old man does not want a young wife on his arm? Besides, I imagine in a few short years, Clarice will be a rich young widow free to do as she pleases. We will have done our parental duty and found her a respectable husband. Beyond that, it is her own affair."

"I see." It was beginning to dawn on Helen that not only was she a burden to her aunt, but her own daughter was not held in much higher esteem.

"As for Lady Arabella, whether she has given up her pursuit of

Tremaine, I cannot say, but I observe that she has become very close to Grand Duke Nicolai Borinsky. Perhaps, having tried the English aristocracy and American adventurers, she is keen to become a member of the Russian royal family." She nodded over to where Arabella was sitting with an older woman, covered in diamonds. "That is his mother, the Princess Maria. If she can charm her, her acceptance in Russian high society is assured."

They sat still for a few moments listening to the soft chatter of the room.

The countess turned her cold gaze back to Helen. "So, it seems that you have played the game and won."

Helen met her eyes. "I have not been playing a game, Aunt. James and I love each other and we want to spend the rest of our lives together trying to make each other happy. Is that so difficult for you to understand?"

Lady Eunice's lips thinned. "You still think love will conquer all? After the disaster that love brought on your own father? Love is something only foolish and naive women believe in while men cloak their lust in words of love. Let me warn you, it does not last. You may believe Tremaine in love with you, and he may even believe it himself, but eventually it will fade with your youth and beauty and then what will you be left with?"

Helen looked steadily at her aunt, wondering what could possibly have happened to have made her so bitter. "If that has been your experience, Aunt, then you have my sympathy, but I do not believe it will be the case for James and me."

"I neither want nor need your sympathy, girl. As I said, you played your cards well, but,"—she paused—"when playing cards, one must not throw away the queen without knowing the whereabouts of the ace."

Helen frowned. "I am sorry, your ladyship, but I do not understand your meaning."

The countess gave a thin smile. "Of course not, but if you wish to know something concerning your mother's blood, you will meet with me tomorrow at Franklin House in Hanover Street."

"I do not believe I know the place."

"There is no reason why you should. Franklin House belongs to me. I inherited it from my mother. I rarely use it, and as it happens it is free of tenants for the moment, so we will be able to meet without the risk of being discovered. There is a need for secrecy and I cannot risk you coming to Rockingham House where the gossip of servants is bound to reach William's ears."

"But why must it be kept from Uncle?"

"Because what I am about to tell you would destroy him. I shall expect you at four tomorrow afternoon. Come in your plainest clothes and tell no one. Do you understand?"

Helen nodded, but could not help the foreboding she felt.

CHAPTER 17

*H*is time with the other men was enjoyable, but he could not help feeling uneasy at leaving Helen with the other women. As soon as he entered the room with the other men, James could tell that he was right, something was troubling his fiancée. He strode over to join her where she was sitting with her aunt. "Are you well, Helen? Your face is very pale."

"I am fine, James, just a little tired, I think." Helen would have died rather than let the countess know how uneasy she felt.

"I was just congratulating my dear Helen on her betrothal, my lord. I heard the wedding is to be in a matter of weeks," the countess said smiling. "I have been chiding Helen about the secrecy of the matter, even from me, but I understand you spoke to my husband and he gave his approval some time ago?"

"Indeed, your ladyship. Lord Rockingham was delighted at our match," James replied. "However, Helen wanted some time to get used to the idea,"—he smiled at her and raised her hand to his lips—"having never expected to marry well." He could not resist adding that.

"How very romantic." Although her words were encouraging, Helen had no doubt from the cold smile and the icy gaze that Lady Eunice was at best angry, and at worst incandescent with rage. "Tell me, my lord, what does your dear mother think of the match? I had assumed that having one unsuitable young lady in the family would be enough."

Now James could see that Helen had endured this sniping since the ladies had retired. "My mother is delighted," he replied with a pleasantness he did not feel. "She was wise enough to realize that, like my brother, I want a wife who is my equal in every sense."

The countess laughed. "Helen will only become your equal on her marriage. Although we have tried to do our best to ensure that she is well-bred, she has no breeding, as I am sure you know. In fact," she said, warming to her subject, "I am surprised that your benefactor, the dear Duke of Bainbridge, has not cautioned you on the dangers of marrying beneath you."

James took a deep breath, but before he could speak, Helen caught his eye. "Pray, do not waste your breath, Lord Tremaine, nothing you can say will make any difference to her ladyship." She rose. "Please excuse me, Countess."

James watched her leave, and then rose as well and leaned toward the older woman, for all appearances, to thank her for coming and bid her farewell. "I believe I know how you hate your niece, and should that become known, it would damage both you and your husband. Frankly, were it only to damage you, I would have no qualms about telling the truth about your 'Christian generosity' here and now as well as publishing it in the scandal sheets for all to see. However, Helen is dearly attached to her uncle and would not wish that embarrassment and shame befall him. So for the moment, you are safe. But," he added quietly, "if word ever gets to me that you have treated or spoken badly about Helen, all will be revealed. I hope I have made myself clear."

The Countess of Rockingham returned his gaze steadily. "Abundantly."

As James walked away, he got the feeling that although he had given a warning, the older woman was not fazed. It was as though she still felt secure in her position over Helen, but what more could she do?

As he walked across the room deep in thought, Arabella appeared in front of him, stopping him abruptly. "I came to congratulate you on your betrothal." She smiled at him. "I genuinely hope that you and Helen will be happy. God knows you both deserve it."

James could not hide his surprise.

Arabella laughed at his expression. "Oh, I know that when I returned, it was my plan to try to go back to where we were. I thought that as you had loved me once, I could make you love me again, but after seeing the two of you together tonight, I see now that I was wrong. You cannot make a person love you, however much you might wish it."

"We are different people now," he said quietly.

"Indeed, we are, and in my case, I truly hope for the better. I hope that one day your brother and Emily will accept that I have changed. They were kind to me when I was desperate after the affair with the diamonds and I let them—and you—down."

"It was a long time ago."

"Well, it would seem that the chances of you running into me in town are getting more remote. My engagement to Nicolai will be announced by the end of the week."

"You are to become a Russian princess?"

"We set sail to Paris next week and will travel through Europe to arrive in St. Petersburg for our wedding in three months' time."

"And how do you communicate? I do not believe you speak Russian."

"Fortunately, Nicolai speaks French, admittedly with the most appalling accent, but we shall get by," she said with bravado.

"And to think it was only days ago you were planning to win me back. I am devastated to be set aside so quickly," he said wryly.

Arabella smiled. "One does what one has to in order to survive. Besides, any fool can see that you are besotted with Helen, and to be frank, I do not think she would have given you up so easily," she admitted.

"Will you not miss life here?"

Arabella took a breath before sighing. "I have few friends here, and those who remember that I jilted you do not consider me worthy of friendship. Frankly, were I to stay here I should never truly regain my place in polite society. Once the novelty of my adventures became less novel, I fear I would end up as a member of the demimonde and that would absolutely kill my parents. I have been given a chance for a fresh start where no one knows me, and I intend to take it. I will not make the same mistake again. Nicolai is not the most exciting man in the world, but he is a good one."

"I hear the weather is dreadfully cold."

Arabella laughed. "You forget that I persevered in the backwoods of America. Have no fear, I am a survivor. Take my advice," she added looking over his shoulder to where Lady Eunice was watching, "ensure that you protect Helen from her monster of an aunt. I may face bears and wolves in Russia, but they are nothing compared to that dragon. Now, I must return to my future mother-in-law. The old lady is a stickler for etiquette and I should not want her to decide that I am suddenly unsuitable, especially," she added with a wink, "as I hope to rightfully inherit those diamonds someday."

*H*elen was glad to have the excuse to sink into the soft cushions of the sofa on the other side of the room from her aunt beside her soon-to-be sister-in-law. "Are you all right?" Emily inquired. "You look rather upset."

"I have just survived a clash with my aunt," Helen explained. "It is rather like wrestling with a crocodile, I imagine."

"She is rather formidable. Lady Tremaine, my mother-in-law, was at school with her and found her to be something of a bully."

"I thought they were bosom friends. That is the impression Lady Eunice gives."

Emily laughed. "Most certainly not. After being tormented for several weeks, Lady Tremaine threw a plant pot at her and scored a bull's-eye apparently. Lady Tremaine is an excellent shot with a pistol, bow and arrow, and a plant pot, it would seem."

"Oh my!" Helen could not help giggling at the thought.

"Of course, the headmistress had to punish Lady Tremaine. One cannot have young ladies attacking each other with plant pots."

"Of course not," Helen agreed.

"I believe she was given a half-hour of sitting in silence to contemplate the error of her ways and she had to clean up the mess. The other mistresses were delighted that someone had finally stood up to her. Apparently, after the incident, Lady Eunice was cured of bullying."

"I see."

"And Lady Eunice carries a slight bump on her nose as a permanent reminder of humility." Emily fanned herself. "I find these rooms terribly hot, would you care to take a stroll around the garden? I believe the duke has it illuminated on these occasions."

Within moments, the two women donned their shawls and were walking arm in arm along the gravel path leading to the lake. As Emily had suggested, the path was well lit. Chinese lanterns hanging from the trees and flares made the garden look like a wonderland. They walked quietly for a minute before Emily broke the silence.

"I am glad of this opportunity to get to know you a little better," Emily began. "Robert and I are delighted that James has at last found the woman who can make him happy."

"I certainly intend to try."

"You know of course about his history with Arabella?"

Helen nodded.

"Then you must know that since then, he has not seriously given another woman consideration. You are the only one he has allowed close."

"I know."

"It took months before he was ready to face society again. Robert and I were worried that he would lose his mind. In fact, I am sure that when he was an officer, he frequently put himself deliberately in harm's way, but," she added, "that is all in the past."

She suddenly stopped walking and faced Helen. "I had better not give you the impression James has been some kind of monk, because he has not. There have been women, but none that he would marry, only those with whom he would share a bed."

Helen was glad of the shadows to hide her blush. "Yes, of course," she said in a small voice.

"Oh, my dear, I have embarrassed you. I do apologize," Emily said quickly. "You do know what happens between a man and his wife, in the marriage bed I mean?"

Helen took a breath. "Not entirely," she admitted. "My mother died when I was very young, and my aunt is not one for intimate conversation, and in school we were told about our duties to bear heirs and our duties to our husbands, but nothing much in...detail," she ended with a blush.

"Then let us rest a moment and I shall tell you the basics." Emily led them to a small stone bench overlooking the lake.

"Knowing James, I am quite certain he has already kissed you."

"Oh, yes, he has made a point of it. He was particularly irritated when I described his kisses as 'merely pleasant.'" Helen laughed.

"That does sound like James." Emily chuckled. "And how do his kisses make you feel?"

Helen thought for a moment, remembering his strong arms around her and his firm lips demanding and giving at the same time. "I just want to be as close to him as I can. I want..." She stopped, not wanting Emily to think her wanton.

"Do you want him to touch you closely and intimately? To consume you, mind and body?" Emily asked without embarrassment.

"Yes, I do. Is that wrong?" Helen asked anxiously.

"Not at all," Emily said hurriedly, reassuringly patting her arm. "On the contrary, it is the most natural and wonderful thing in the world."

"Oh, thank goodness, I was beginning to feel that I was unnatural." Helen sighed with relief.

"On your wedding night, and many other nights I am sure, James will come to you. He will want to remove all your clothing, or watch you do so, and although this seems strange, trust me, it will be very enjoyable for both of you. Then he will want to look at your body and touch you, not only with his hands, but his mouth. He will want to touch every part of you, and believe me, my dear," she said with a smile as she patted Helen's knee, "you will be more than happy for him to do so. Eventually, he will part your legs and touch your womanhood. Do not be alarmed at this, the feeling is quite wonderful. When he is ready, and I am sure he will ensure that you are ready as well, he will lie on top of you and enter you with his male member. This is the most exciting part of all... Oh dear," she said, looking at Helen's puzzled face. "I do not think I have done justice to what is the most special part of lovemaking."

"This is the part I do not understand," Helen admitted, nervously intrigued.

"You know of course that a man has a different..."—she paused for the right word to come to mind—"...shape?"

"You mean the appendage? I have seen babies before, but I am sure it must be different on a man."

For a second, Emily was nonplussed, but she quickly regained her composure. "Exactly so. Now, when a man is aroused, it becomes hard and large..." Emily paused, looking as if she was beginning to regret ploughing into this conversation.

"That's what I feel when James holds me close?"

"Indeed, now that is what he will put inside you, when he has made sure you are ready, and you will move together. It is difficult to explain, but when two bodies meet and move together to make love, the feeling is exquisite. Just let me reassure you that it is the most wonderful feeling," Emily said quickly, almost eager now to end this.

"And this is the mystery of the wedding night?"

"Well, it is not just the wedding night. Husbands and wives do this a lot, whenever they wish. You must trust me on this, I am sure that James will be a wonderful lover and will ensure that you enjoy this aspect of marriage as Robert does with me. And," she added, resting her hand lightly on her stomach, "the most wonderful thing is that this sometimes results in a baby."

CHAPTER 18

As she settled into the squabs later that night, Helen thought about what the young duchess had told her. She made the decision that, should she have the opportunity, she would ensure that James made love to her. Somehow, she knew her meeting with her aunt the following day was not going to be a happy one. For some reason, Lady Eunice would move Heaven and Earth to ensure that she was either ruined or that her marriage to James would not take place. Yet she had to go. The possibility that she might learn something of her own blood relatives was too appealing. She was desperate to know anything about them.

Unable to sleep, Helen had just padded down to the library to get a book when she heard a noise. Taking the candlestick, she followed the noise to the door at the bottom of the stairs outside of the kitchen. When she opened the door and saw who it was, she almost dropped the candle. James was sitting at the scrubbed table helping himself to a hearty slice of bread and a slab of cheese.

"James, what are you doing?"

"Having supper," he replied between mouthfuls.

"I meant, what are you doing here?"

"I came to see you. You were fine during the dinner, but when I saw you after port, you were distracted and could not settle. I know your aunt said something to distress you."

"Are you mad, coming here in the middle of the night?"

"Possibly," he said and laughed.

"Foxed?"

"I would remind you that I am a gentleman and a gentleman can always take his drink, but no, I am not foxed."

"You do realize that if anyone found you here, I would be ruined?"

James suddenly became serious. "You know that is the last thing I would do. I would tear my own heart out rather than see you hurt."

Helen could not help but smile. "Hopefully it will not need to come to that."

James grinned. "Then perhaps you might do me the honour of joining me for a late supper. Your grandmother does keep a fine stock of cheese."

Helen shook her head in disbelief at the thought of having a conversation with her fiancé in her grandmother's kitchen in the pre-dawn morning on the subject of cheese. "You seem remarkably adept at finding your way around a kitchen," she commented.

"I learned my foraging skills early on in the army, though I admit that your grandmother's cook made the expedition reasonably easy."

"It would appear that someone else also made your expedition easy as well. How did you get in?"

He did have the decency to look a little sheepish. "Talbot, your grandmother's footman, was most helpful."

Helen was alarmed. "If he was happy to let you in, how do I know that he would not do the same for someone else—a burglar, or someone intent on doing us harm?"

"I can assure you that Talbot adores your grandmother and would lay his life down to protect her, and if I upset you I am fairly sure he will take great pleasure in tearing me apart limb from limb," he told her. "He only let me in because he also noticed that you arrived home subdued and was worried about you. Now, will you tell me what it is?"

Helen thought for a moment. If she told him what her aunt had said about information about her blood family, he would insist on accompanying her and she had no doubt that her aunt would not only refuse to reveal what she knew, she would ensure that Helen never found out what she so desperately wanted to know. "My aunt was merely insistent on knowing everything about the wedding," she replied, knowing it sounded feeble even to her own ears. "She does not approve of the modiste who is making the gown, nor the church, nor the menu for the wedding breakfast. You know how women are regarding weddings, and my aunt in particular is not a woman who likes to be crossed," she added, comfortable that the last was, at least, the truth.

James carefully schooled his features to appear relaxed before responding, doing his best to sound convinced. From what he knew of Lady Rockingham, she would not have left Helen so disturbed by merely arguing about the frippery of the wedding. She must have done more to have upset Helen so much that Talbot granted him access to the house. "Is that all? Then I have a solution to the problem. I can get a special license tomorrow and we can have the wedding here or privately at my house two days hence. If, of course, that is what you want."

Helen smiled. "In truth, a small wedding would suit me, but my grandmother is having so much fun arranging things, I should not like to take the pleasure away from her."

"Then I shall arrange for the license. To be used if necessary." He grinned. "I also saw you in cahoots with my sister-in-law. She was not encouraging unladylike behavior, I trust?"

Helen raised an eyebrow. "Our conversation was most instructive."

"About what? The duties of a duchess? Music? Art? I would suggest gowns, bonnets, and jewels, but as I know these interest neither of you, I doubt they were discussed."

"As a matter of fact, Emily was explaining to me the duties of the marriage bed."

There was a pause while James recovered from a choking fit, then he replaced his bread on the plate and took a swig of wine. "And was it instructive?" he could not help himself asking.

"Very," she replied, sweeping the remnants of his supper to one side and sitting on the table in front of him. "It certainly answered some of my questions."

"Such as?" he probed, knowing that he was maintaining his self-control on the barest of threads and the slightest provocation might push him to take her on the table, there and then. Still, he could recognize that Helen was enjoying teasing him with the sexual conversation. The timid Miss Nobody was discovering the power of her sexuality and he loved it.

"Well," she said, leaning back slightly, and playing with the ribbons fastening her nightrail. "I had not realized quite how much a man would enjoy looking at a naked woman, though I suppose all those paintings of nymphs and goddesses should have given me a clue. Their owners were more interested in naked women than classical myths I imagine."

"I imagine they were," he agreed.

"Of course I have never been seen by a man," she said as she slowly drew the ribbons apart and her nightrail slid from her shoulders.

"I can assure you that if you continue, you shortly will be," he growled.

"Would you like that?" Her voice was low and husky.

"I think you know I would." His voice was thick with desire. "But I must warn you, Miss, you are playing with fire." He rose shakily to his feet and slowly circled the room to ensure each door was securely latched. He could feel her eyes watching him and the heat emanating from her, pulling him toward her.

"Then perhaps it's time I started a blaze," she challenged.

James leaned forward and took her mouth in a slow, drugging kiss as he slowly pulled all the ribbons apart and eased her nightrail from her body before leaning back to look at her.

"Part your legs for me, I want to see all of you," he directed, eyes bright with fervor.

Fascinated by his reaction, Helen obeyed and leaned back.

His eyes hungrily raked down her body, taking in the curve of her shoulder, her small but full breasts, and narrow waist before dropping to her belly and lower to the neat, dark curls between her legs. "God, you are perfect," he breathed, "never be ashamed of your body as some women are taught to be."

"Do you like what you see?" she asked softly.

"Unquestionably," he breathed as he reached forward and stroked a finger along her breast, delighting in the instant tightening of her nipple and the gasp his touch elicited from her. "Now, my little wanton minx, I think it is only fair that you learn the next lesson in seduction, which the dear duchess may not have covered. Once a man has seen, he will always want to touch."

He cupped her face with both hands and kissed her, his tongue demanding and receiving entry to her mouth, plunging in and out as his hands slipped lower to caress her breasts, his thumbs circling her nipples until she cried out with need.

"We have only just begun, my sweet," he murmured as his mouth replaced his hands and laving thoroughly one breast and then the other while his hands stroked her body, keeping her pressed against him.

Helen could scarcely breathe. All thoughts left her head, all she was aware of were the myriad feelings in her body as James touched her. Nor could she stop the involuntary gasps and moans as his hands ever so slowly drifted lower. She almost shot off the table as his tongue traced the outline of her feminine core. Once again, his wonderful tongue delved in and out as he found her nub and stroked it mercilessly until she thought she was going to die of pleasure. As she began to feel wave after wave of intimate pleasure wash over her, he covered her mouth with his own, breathing in her moans until she was sure she would die consumed by pleasure. He gathered her shaking body in his arms, kissing the top of her head and gentling her as she returned to her surroundings.

She turned her head to look at him. "I have never known myself to be capable of feeling such pleasure, James. Should I now do something for you to experience the same?"

"Oh, I fully intend that you shall make up for the pleasure deficit, my love, but I will not make love to you on a kitchen table like some randy serving boy. For your first time, it will be in a bed with silk sheets."

She blushed a deep red as her mind cleared and she fully realized what she had done. "You must think me beyond forward now. I hope you are not disappointed by my impropriety," she whispered, embarrassed.

"I find you delightful, darling." He cupped her chin and looked into her eyes. "I cannot tell you how pleased I am to find that you and I will match each other in every way, but I have to tell you that I do not want to wait any longer to make you mine. I shall obtain a special license and we shall be married before the sun sets twice more, before I go completely insane."

"But what about Grandmama and her plans for the wedding?"

"Believe me, when we present her with her first great-grandchild, she will forgive us, and I cannot imagine she will have to wait long." He chuckled. "Now, off to bed with you before I forget that I am a gentleman."

As he let himself out, it occurred to him that he had come to find out what her aunt had said to distress her, and he was certain she had not told him. He shrugged. In two days they would be married, and she need never worry about her poisonous aunt again.

CHAPTER 19

*H*elen took a deep breath as the hackney carriage turned onto Hanover Street. She was relieved she had not needed to lie to her grandmother. Fortunately, the dowager had announced over breakfast that she was going to visit her friend, and as Lady Walton lived out toward Hampton Court, would Helen mind if she stayed for the night. It was irregular for a young woman to be left on her own, but her grandmother believed her to be a sensible girl, and after all, what harm could she come to in one night?

What harm indeed? Helen thought as she stepped from the carriage. She had done as her aunt had commanded and worn one of her old dresses, a drab affair in brown, with a large brimmed bonnet that did a fine job of almost completely hiding her face. Anyone seeing her would have thought she was a young woman coming for an interview for the post of governess. She looked up at the facade, surprised by the size and grandeur of Franklin House. It was built in the modern classical style with three stories of family rooms with elegant windows and steps which she assumed led to the cellar.

She was surprised when her aunt opened the door herself and beckoned her inside. "Come quickly, girl. Do not dawdle in the street for all the neighbours to see." Helen was ushered into a small sitting room where all but two chairs by the white marble fireplace and a small side table were covered in dust sheets. The older woman gestured her to sit down.

Helen was intrigued. "I am at a loss to know why there is a need for such secrecy, Aunt, just for you to tell the story of my family. Other than me, there is no one left who would be remotely interested."

"I can assure you, young woman, that when you have heard what I have to say, you will understand exactly why this must be kept secret."

"Very well." Helen looked expectantly at her aunt.

"Before I tell you anything, I require you to give me your solemn oath, that nothing I say will be repeated to another living soul."

"Of course not."

"Do you swear it?"

"I swear it."

"There is something else, payment if you will," her aunt began.

Helen shook her head. "I have no money with me, Aunt."

The older woman laughed. "I do not require your money, Helen. In addition to your silence on this matter you will be required to leave London immediately."

Helen reared back. She had not expected this. "I do not understand," she stammered.

"There is no reason why you should," her aunt agreed. "However, my price for this information is that you leave London immediately and do not return."

"Aunt Eunice, you know that I am about to marry," she reasoned.

"Ah, yes, the wedding to the dashing marquess. I am afraid that will not be taking place."

"But everything is arranged, you were at the betrothal dinner only last night," she said, feeling as if the dinner was a lifetime ago.

"And that is why we are having this little chat today before your scheme goes any further," her aunt said smoothly.

Helen froze before rising slowly from her seat. "I am leaving now. I believe you are quite mad. There is nothing you can tell me about my blood family, who in any case are all dead, for which I would consider sacrificing my marriage to Lord Tremaine."

Just as her hand touched the door, the countess called, "So you do not wish to know the whereabouts of your brother?"

Helen whirled round, her face drained of colour. "What are you saying, Aunt? I have no brother. I have no living blood relatives other than my uncle and Clarice."

"And if you go through that door, you will never know," Eunice said sharply, her eyes glittering with malice.

There was silence as Helen tried to gather her thoughts into order. If what her aunt suggested was true, she had a brother. On the other hand, her aunt could be lying, and she would be sacrificing lifetime happiness with James for a wild goose chase.

"Why should I believe you?" she asked.

"Can you afford not to?" her aunt countered. She patted the chair beside her. "Now stop being foolish and sit down."

Helen walked slowly back and stood by the seat, ready to flee.

"If what you say is true and I have a brother, why must it cost me my marriage to James?"

"Life is full of difficult choices, my dear, you now have to make yours. If you choose your life with James, you will never know about your brother. It is a secret I will take with me to my grave. I am the only one who knows about both the boy and his whereabouts. If, on the other hand, you choose to learn about your brother, I will provide for you both to live in a cottage with sufficient means to allow you to live in a degree of comfort for the rest of your lives. The question you must ask yourself, is the price worth paying to find the family you have always wished for."

"But why? Why must it cost my marriage? Why, when I found a man I love and who loves me and finally have the chance of happiness, must you try to take it away from me?" Helen was bewildered.

Her aunt's eyes were as cold and hard as ice. "Because your mother took away my chance of happiness. Now, make your choice."

It was as though the life she could have had flashed before her eyes—James promising to love and cherish her, bearing his child and seeing his joy, waking up with him each morning, having dinner with him each night...the anguish she knew he would feel when he was left by another woman before his wedding. She remembered what his mother said, that the last time had all but destroyed him. Could she live with herself knowing she had caused him so much pain? Could she live with the pain and doubt of abandoning her only family for the rest of her life? Her aunt knew her Achilles heel, she knew that all her life Helen had longed for a real family.

She could not stop the tears from falling as she sat, once again feeling defeated by her aunt's power over her life. "Please tell me about my brother."

Her aunt's face was triumphant as she said, "You agree to my terms?"

"For the love of God, why cannot you just tell me?"

"Because I have waited a long time for my revenge. Now, do you agree to my terms?"

Helen nodded.

The countess's face relaxed. "What do you remember of your early life, before you came to live with us?"

"I was happy when Papa was alive, when we lived close to my grandparents. I remember feeling afraid when I was in the poorhouse. Grandmother died, and my mother was ill and weak. There was never enough food."

"Do you remember what happened when your mother died?"

"They just said my mother died having the baby and that the baby would not long follow her. They found the letter and the teaspoons she had somehow managed to keep. The warden washed me and brought me to Rockingham the next day. I think she thought there might be some money in it for her."

"Indeed," her aunt said. "But the child survived, beyond all expectations."

"Why was he not brought to Rockingham as I was?"

"Because when I was told, I refused to be saddled with yet another unwanted child I most certainly did not want to bring up."

Helen shook her head in disbelief. "What made you so cold against us, your ladyship?"

The Countess of Rockingham laughed. "I suppose you are owed an explanation, as I will probably never see you again. You once asked me what you had done to make me hate you. The fact is I hate you not for what you have done or what you are, but for *who* you are." She paused for a moment, her eyes misting. "I was once betrothed to your father. Our parents had agreed on the matter and the marriage contract had been signed. For Jonathon, it was an arranged marriage, as many society marriages are, and I knew he did not love me as I loved him, but I knew I could make him love me in time. And I would have," she added fiercely, "had he not been bewitched by your mother."

"My mother?" Helen repeated.

"She was a beauty, I grant you, even though she was lowborn. In fact, every time I look at you, I see her." Eunice paused for a moment, lost in the memory of a lost past. "Jonathon was obsessed with engineering, he had little interest in the appropriate pastimes of a gentleman. He was never happier than when he was building some kind of mechanical object and began going down to his father's mine against the old earl's wishes, but he did not stop him, thinking it would be a phase he would soon come through. He would return singing the praises of the mine manager who had designed machines to improve the conditions of the miners, something his father had never considered. Landowners rarely bothered themselves with such details. Jonathon began spending more and more time with the manager and the miners until one day his father told him the visits must stop, he was to stop behaving like a common person and behave like a gentleman.

"Jonathon refused, telling his father that any number of miners were better men than so-called gentlemen who lived lives of idle selfishness. He had also fallen in love with the mine manager's daughter and intended to break our engagement to marry her. At this point, the earl cut him off without a penny." She paused for a moment and wiped her eyes.

"I am sorry, Aunt, I had no idea." Helen could not reveal she knew her grandpapa had not finally cut off his son for fear her aunt would refuse to tell her of her brother.

"Of course not," Eunice snapped. "The betrothal, unlike yours, had not been formally announced. Jonathon came to see me, at least he had the courage to tell me to my face. Do you know what I was doing when he arrived?" She laughed her mirthless laugh once more. "I was looking through the Paris fashion prints for a design for my wedding dress." Helen leaned forward and patted her aunt's hand, but her hand was quickly shaken off. "Jonathon requested a moment alone with me. I with my head full of romance, thought he had come to declare his love, which he had, but not for me. He explained that he had fallen in love with Molly, the mine manager's daughter, and could not go through with our wedding. He intended to marry her. I cried and screamed and even offered that if he married me he could take this Molly person as his mistress, but nothing I did made any difference. He was adamant that having found love, he would not settle for less than marriage. It was the last time I saw him."

"But how did you come to marry my uncle? Do marriages of this kind not take time to negotiate?"

"The matter was decided by our fathers. The contract had been signed, the marriage had always been intended to unite our lands. All that mattered was that our families were joined, so the only change was the name on the contract. So Jonathon was disinherited and William made heir. I would still be marrying a future earl, although," she added, "I never came to love William. We have tolerated each other all these years, but we both knew it was second best. Once I had Clarice and it became obvious we could not have more children, your uncle and I have led our own lives."

"I am so sorry, Aunt Eunice."

The older woman stiffened her spine. "I do not need your sympathy. I have looked forward to the day I would be able to exact revenge on your mother for stealing the life that should have been mine. Since she died and robbed me of the opportunity, it is now your turn to suffer in her stead. As I was denied the man I loved by your mother, so shall you be by me, rather a neat ending to the story, do not you think?"

Helen began to feel prickles of alarm, although she now understood in some way her aunt's bitterness and it explained her ill treatment over the years. The older woman's obsession with revenge was far from healthy. Even after twenty years the hurt and anger seemed as fresh as it had been at the time.

The countess suddenly took a deep breath and seemed to strengthen from her victory. "And now I shall tell you about your brother."

CHAPTER 20

*H*elen waited as her aunt took a breath. She could hardly contain herself. After all these years of thinking that she had no one, to find that she had a brother was incredible. Of course, he would be almost a young man by now, but she could not wait to meet him.

"It is true that your mother died of childbed fever not long after giving birth to your brother. According to the warden, there was no midwife—some of the other women tried to help but the birth was not easy. Your mother deteriorated very quickly."

"Did she know she had a son?"

"I believe so. And normally that would have been the end of that. You and your little brother would have been apprenticed to some local tradesman, or lived your lives out in the poorhouse, but for those damned spoons."

"The teaspoons? The ones my grandmother gave to my father as he left?"

"Exactly so. When they were washing your mother's body for burial, one of the women found the spoons and the letter. I imagine your mother had sewn them into her clothing in some way. The woman reported her findings to the warden who recognized the crest. She was also no doubt aware of the story of the disinherited son and thought there might be a reward for reuniting you with your family."

A long forgotten memory surfaced in Helen's mind. "Mrs. White, she told me I was to tell you how well-fed and treated we were should you ask." Not that Eunice had bothered.

The countess continued as though Helen had not spoken. "When you arrived at Rockingham, it was a tremendous shock. We knew, of course, that Jonathon had kept his word and married your mother, but the old earl forbade even the mention of his name until his dying day. We had no idea there were children. As I told you, had my husband been out when you arrived, I would have ensured that you were removed, and he would have been none the wiser. I knew at once you were Jonathon's daughter. You are the image of your mother, but you have his eyes," she said in disgust.

"And my brother?" Helen prompted.

"The White woman assured me that the baby was a sickly thing and would not last the week, yet against all odds he did, and the woman sent a message to tell me he had recovered and had started to thrive. I arranged to see her and persuaded her that the child must be adopted and taken to a distant location. She said she knew a couple who wanted a child and agreed to make the necessary arrangements. We agreed a sum of money and the problem was solved."

"But why could you not take in my brother as well as myself?"

"I did not want you at all! I had to take you because William insisted. Fortunately, William did not know the child survived. He still does not and will not."

"I do not understand you, my lady. I do not understand how you could turn your back on a helpless babe."

"Looking at you each day would be reminder enough of what your mother stole from me. To be forced to raise the son that Jonathan had with another woman was something I would never allow myself to do. To raise that woman's son when I could have none of my own was a cruelty I could not bear. Knowing that you have failed to produce an heir is a pain that never heals. My only chance was for Clarice to marry well and as I watched you grow, I saw that you would outshine her, just as your mother outshone me. Well, I would not allow the injustice to be done in two generations. Though I could not punish her, I could punish you, and that has been my consolation."

Helen paused for a moment to let all her aunt said wash over her. Her aunt was quite mad, of that she was sure, and Eunice's obsession with her mother over the years had completely taken her senses. But she still needed to know about her brother. "You said Mrs. White arranged for my brother to be adopted," she prompted.

"Before I say more, I would remind you of our agreement. At first light, two days hence, you will travel alone to be with your brother. I will send a message ahead so that you will be expected. Is that understood?"

Helen nodded.

"You will not communicate your whereabouts to anyone, nor will you give prior warning of your departure."

Helen's head shot up. "But what of Grandmama? And if I am to leave James…surely I must be able to tell him why I am leaving? Surely, Aunt, you cannot be so cruel as to allow him to believe he has been left callously a second time."

Eunice smiled mirthlessly once more. "But that is the beauty of my plan, dear. Tremaine will hate you. I want you to know how it feels to lose the one man you love. As to your grandmother, she has interfered in my life for the last time. I shall deal with her." She folded her hands neatly. "Those are my terms. Either accept them or accept that you will never see your brother."

Helen had once more been boxed in by her aunt. She had little option, but somehow, she would find a way through. She had to. "Very well, my lady, you leave me with little choice."

The older woman eyed her for a long moment before saying, "Your brother has been brought up in Whitby. He attends the grammar school and soon he will be apprenticed at the local bank. A bright boy by all accounts."

"But who looks after him?"

"I have provided a cottage and some yearly funds to the couple who took him. He has not been raised in luxury, but neither has he been neglected."

"Why did you bother if you resented us both so much?" Helen asked bitterly.

"I should not want the death of a child on my conscience."

"Is it not a little late to worry about your conscience now?"

The countess actually looked thoughtful. "We all make choices. Sometimes the choices are limited and sometimes others make the choices for us. I have no doubt that I shall have to account for mine one day, but until then…" She paused, opened her reticule, and handed Helen a piece of paper. "Here is the address. I shall send an unmarked hansom for you at first light. You will travel first to Smithfield, where you will board the stagecoach for York. Once there, you will change for the coach to Whitby—there are several each week. You will meet your brother within the week. Here is your ticket and some money to pay for whatever necessaries you might need on the journey."

Helen took the ticket. "You were very sure I would accept your offer."

"I knew you would not be able to resist the opportunity of a link with your past. There is just one thing more," the older woman said, indicating the table beside her chair. You will sign this paper promising to uphold your part of our agreement."

"Do you not trust me aunt?" Helen asked.

Her aunt's eyes narrowed as she watched Helen sign, "I have learned to trust no-one, least of all you. Your mother cheated me once, I do not intend that history repeats itself. Now," the Countess of Rockingham said tucking the paper into her reticule as she stood, "I think our business is finished here."

*W*hen she returned home, Helen was relieved to find a message from her grandmother which said that she would be staying a further three nights. It was heartening to know that she would not have to live a lie for three days and heartbreaking to know that she would, in all probability, never see her grandmother again. Even if by chance they should ever meet, she doubted the dowager would ever forgive her. She was even more worried about how James would react to her departure. He certainly would never forgive her after his experience with Arabella—Lady Eunice was absolutely right about that— and she doubted he would ever view a woman favourably again. He would marry and produce the requisite heirs, of that she was sure, but would he ever give his heart again? She doubted it, and whether she had irreparably broken his heart or if he went on to find love again would be her pain to bear.

She was grateful that a meeting with Mr. Thompson had already been arranged. He raised his eyebrows when she requested that all future monies were to be paid to Pearse's Bank in Whitby but was pleased to tell her that her book was almost ready for publication. He was disappointed for her desire to be published anonymously as he believed that a titled lady writing a book was guaranteed to sell more copies, but he was sympathetic when she said that she needed to go to the seaside for the benefit of her health and promised to keep her location secret. He was delighted to learn that she was well on her way to finishing her second book and had ideas for a third. It was now imperative that she earn her own money, for although her aunt had promised to pay for her and her brother, she could not rely on her aunt's frame of mind.

That night, she still felt sick to her stomach at the thought of what was to come.

"Are you feeling well, Miss?" Lucy broke into her reverie as she sat while the maid dressed her hair. "You seem a bit pale and quiet."

Helen forced a smile to her lips. "I am well, thank you, Lucy, just a little tired, I think," she lied. The last thing she wanted was to go to the theatre, but she knew she must carry on as normal if no one was to guess that in three days she would be gone from their lives forever. As Lucy pinned the final few pearls in place, she regarded her reflection in the mirror. The deep blue trim contrasted the pale blue of the silk emphasizing the colour of her eyes. Once again, Lucy had tamed her chestnut curls, sweeping her hair into a loose chignon from which one or two tendrils had been teased. Anyone looking at her would see a beautiful, confident young woman on the verge of a new life with her handsome husband. She sighed. She was certainly on the verge of a new life, but it was not the one she had imagined two days ago. No one looking at her would guess that beneath the silk and pearls, her heart was breaking.

She sat through the play mindlessly, laughing when the rest of the audience laughed and when they clapped, she did the same. All her thoughts were on the handsome man beside her who would never forgive her for what she was about to do to him. Even if he understood her desperate need to know her brother, he would never forget or forgive her for doing what Arabella did and she could not blame him. She glanced at Lady Tremaine, who had come as their chaperone. None of the Tremaines would ever associate with her again. In gaining a family of her blood, she would lose the family who had taken her to their hearts.

As they gathered their things at the end of the performance, Lady Tremaine asked her son, "Would you mind if I travelled with the Macleans? I had quite forgotten that Maclean's brother has arrived from the continent. He was a dear friend of your father's." She waved her hand. "I know it is a little irregular for you to be left alone together, but as you are to be man and wife in a matter of weeks, I cannot think that there should be a scandal."

"Of course not, Mother," James replied, knowing that the license in his pocket meant that he and Helen would in fact be married even sooner. His mother smiled as she hurried off to meet her friends.

When the carriage rolled to a halt, Helen was surprised to find it was standing outside James' mansion. He turned to her. "Before you go home, there is something I want you to see." Helen looked doubtful.

"I assure you, no one will know you have been, most of the servants are in bed and those who are not are more than discreet. Besides," he added, "you need only stay a moment." He jumped lightly down from the carriage and held out his hand.

She eyed him skeptically. "Just for a moment," she said before climbing down.

They were obviously expected, as a cheerful fire blazed in the grate and a decanter of sherry and shortbread biscuits sat on the small table. The sitting room was intimate with the walls covered in duck-egg blue damask, darker blue drapes covering the long windows, a pianoforte at one end, and a writing desk by the window. It was a wonderful, beautiful room she could imagine them spending their evenings in, and it broke her heart that there would be no cozy, intimate evenings in this room. After she left tonight, there would be no evenings together at all.

"I hope you like it." He gestured. "I had it decorated for you. I thought you might like a room for yourself for your writing and so on," he explained, moving toward the writing desk.

"It's lovely," she responded, struggling to keep her voice even. "Quite perfect." Helen's heart was breaking. His thoughtfulness and generosity was about to be shattered by her disloyalty, no matter the reason, and he and all society would view it in the same way. Her aunt had won. When she left to meet her brother, she would be eternally labeled pariah.

"This is what I wanted you to see," James said eagerly, as he strode forward holding out a small package. "Open it."

She took it from him with trembling fingers and opened it slowly to find a gold locket. He watched her closely as she coaxed the clasp open. Her eyes shot to his. "It is a miniature of your father," he explained.

"But how did you? How could you? I have never seen this before."

He smiled down at her, knowing that if he had given her a suite of diamonds, they would not have impressed her nearly as much. "I enlisted your uncle's help. I knew as heir to an earldom your father must have had his portrait painted at some time. I asked your uncle, who distinctly remembered the painting. Apparently, your aunt had it put in storage at the castle when your grandmother left to live in the Dower House. Your uncle brought it down and I had a copy made for this locket, though we shall hang the original in this room, I think. I am sorry," he added, "that there is nothing of your mother."

"My aunt says I am the image of my mother," Helen replied softly.

"But look here," he said pointing into the locket, "I can see your father in you also. Now, let's put it on. A locket is meant to be worn."

As he fastened it around her neck, he could not resist placing a kiss just below her ear. Helen turned in his arms and pulled his head down to hers in a searing kiss that left them both breathless. He crushed her to him wanting to feel her body against his, his lips closed over hers, his tongue seeking and finding entrance to her mouth. His hands roamed restlessly over her back, cupping her bottom, and pulling her even closer so that she could feel his hard length against her.

He raised his head, gasping. "I apologize, Helen, that should not have happened. I promise you, I had no intention of ravishing you when I brought you here. I only wanted to give you the locket."

He could see her eyes were dark with passion and her lips were swollen from his kisses.

"What if I want to be ravished?" she asked softly.

He took a sharp intake of breath. "You do not mean that, we are to be married in a few days. I can wait a little longer."

She pulled his head down again. "But I cannot," she whispered before taking his lips again. If all she was to have was one night with James to remember for the rest of her life, she wanted to take it. She wanted to know what making love with the only man she would ever love was to be like. She wanted *him*. "Besides, we are to be married in a matter of hours, what difference can it make?" she reasoned, her eyes pleading with him, wearing him down.

James looked at her. "If you are sure."

"I am sure. I want you to make love to me as only you can," she responded evenly, locking his gaze.

"Then who am I to deny you? I can barely resist myself, but I cannot resist you. Come, darling. I have a place much more comfortable for this." His heart beating and his body burning at her touch, he took her hand and guided her up the stairs to his bedchamber. A canopied bed stood on a dais at the end of the room, and a fire burned in the marble fireplace. Helen turned and surveyed the room as James closed and locked the door behind them. The room was well-lit with candelabras on the tallboys and tables, the windows were hung with rich red, velvet drapes. James stood by the door, hand on the latch, watching her. "Are you certain?"

"I am. More certain of this than anything in my life."

"Then the time for talking is over."

He was at her side in an instant, grasping her to his long, hard body. Helen held him willingly, her joy at finally being with James overcoming any modesty she knew she should have been feeling. Her hands caressed his back while he quickly dispensed with the pins holding her hair in place so that he could run his fingers through it. "So soft," he muttered as his hands went to the back of her frock and quickly unfastened the buttons. Within a heartbeat, her dress was in a pool at her feet. Her petticoat and chemise soon followed, and she stood before him in her stockings. Slowly, he bent and undid the ribbons holding up her stockings and rolled them down her legs, kissing her flesh as he did so.

Helen's skin tingled pleasantly, and she felt a tightening within her. She made no move to cover her nakedness. She had learned from her experience a few days ago that James enjoyed looking at her.

He took a step back, just to look at her. The way she stood there shamelessly, looking him in the eye made his body throb almost painfully. He was in awe of this woman. "You are so beautiful," he whispered, feeling inadequate. He reached out a hand to lightly stroke her breast and her nipple tightened instantly at his touch. "And you are mine," he growled possessively, the need to make it true taking over his body. He pulled her to him, crushing her body against his, before he lifted her and laid her on the bed. Without taking his eyes off her, he quickly shed his jacket and neckcloth and dragged his shirt over his head.

Helen's eyes feasted on his tightly muscled torso, realizing now that the cold marble of statues in museums could not compare to the living flesh. His chest was finely covered with dark hair which whorled around his pink, flat, nipples and trailed in a line down the front of his breeches. She could not help but reach out and trace a finger down the fine hairs, though at his groan, she snatched her hand back as though scalded.

"I am sorry," she stammered. "I did not mean to hurt you."

He grinned. "Far from it, you know the pleasure you have when I touch you?" She nodded. "Your touch pleasures me more than I could tell you," he explained with a chuckle.

"Ah,"—she smiled—"then let me pleasure you as you have pleasured me."

She reached for him, but he stilled her hand. "Sweetheart, if you give me any more pleasure, I might just expire on this bed. Tonight is about you. I want you to relax and give yourself over to me. I will do all I can to give you the greatest pleasure possible. I have to warn you that there may be a moment of pain for you and if I could take it for you I would, but once that barrier is passed, you should feel nothing but pleasure. Just put your trust in me."

Helen nodded. "I trust you, James. I love you. Whatever happens, know that I love you."

James needed no further bidding. His mouth came down on hers in a demanding kiss as his hands teased and caressed her breasts. His mouth moved lower, sucking and laving the sensitive buds until she was writhing beneath him. As his mouth gave attention to her breasts, his fingers sought her slick opening, dipping in and out, searching for and finding the small nub and circling it. Helen could not help the soft cries in her throat as every cell in her body responded to his touch; she felt she was going to come apart in his hands.

"James," she gasped.

He raised his head. "What is it, my love?"

"I cannot help but notice that while I am completely naked, you are still wearing your breeches...is there some point at which they come off?" she asked breathlessly, still managing to raise an eyebrow at him.

"You are right." He laughed softly. "I did not want my nakedness to scare you, but it is time." In a fluid movement, he shucked off his breeches.

Helen's eyes widened; now she knew where the line of hair ended. He was magnificent, a true specimen of the glory of the male physique. "You are so handsome," she murmured, taking in his long muscular legs and proud member. She had never seen one in this state and was interested to explore it. "May I?" she asked, reaching out.

"I should like it very much if you do," he replied breathlessly, his heart nearly stopping as he watched her reach out.

Helen touched him gently, slowly grasping him in her hand. "It is silky, yet hard as iron," she said, surprised.

He closed his eyes, praying for strength to remain calm. "That is what you do to me, love, and now we need to finish what we started before I am unable to please you as you deserve."

He shifted her legs and raised himself above her before entering her slowly, letting her body get used to him. When he'd progressed as much as he could easily, he came to the place where he would need to break her body's natural defenses. "I am sorry, my love," he whispered as he drove forward kissing her. He felt her tense and he froze, allowing her body to adjust to his member stretching her as she had never been.

It was mere seconds before he felt her walls tightening around him and he began to move inside her.

Helen instinctively matched his thrusts until she felt tension building inside. Her whole body was tingling with fire as the passion overwhelmed her, and she could scarcely breathe. She felt truly alive for the first time. The tension became almost unbearable and then it was as though a huge cloud burst and tremor after tremor washed over her.

James felt her tremors before his own climax and his groan covered her whimpers of pleasure and need. When they were both still, the only sound in the room was their breathing as it returned to normal. James lay beside her and gathered her in his arms. "My God, Helen, I have never felt like this before. I shall never get enough of you, darling, never. God…this is what making love is truly about."

Helen snuggled closer. "I had no idea," she breathed. "I thought I was going to die of pleasure. Do all women feel this way? I cannot imagine it being deemed as appropriate."

"Not all women are as responsive as you." James laughed. "Some just see it as a duty, something they must go through for the getting of heirs, however, we are fortunate as we will not only love each other until death, but we shall spend many happy hours enjoying ourselves in the getting of heirs."

At his words, Helen could not help a tear running down her face.

"What's this, love? Why are you crying?" he asked, his voice concerned. "I hope you are not regretting what we have done."

She shook her head. "How could I regret that? You have made me the happiest of women." It was not a lie. James had made her happy, but only she knew that after tonight there would be no more making love. After tonight, she would never see him again.

CHAPTER 21

For the second time in a week, Helen found herself in a closed carriage arranged by her aunt. It had arrived just before dawn to take her to Charing Cross where she would board the coach for York and then on to Whitby to meet her brother. She had only a small valise containing her simplest clothes for there would be no need for any of the beautiful gowns James had purchased for her. From almost being a duchess, she would be living a life of obscurity. Her income from her writing would help to ensure that they lived comfortably, if not with a great degree of luxury.

As the coach twisted and turned through the narrow streets out of the capital, her thoughts returned to James and the night they had shared. After their initial lovemaking, he had reached for her again during the night and once more before she had to leave. He had helped her to dress and drove her to her grandmother's before any of the servants were up. He waited until he saw candlelight in her room before driving away. His parting words were seared on her soul: "I will never get enough of you. I cannot wait for the few hours to pass so that I can make you my wife, and then nothing can ever separate us again." She would never forget that night, those memories had to last a lifetime, there would be no one else. Some might be able to love more than once, but she knew she could only love once and the only man she could love was James.

She had heeded her aunt's words and left without a note, but she decided that when she reached York, she would send him a brief letter, not explaining where she was or why she had left, but she would ask for his forgiveness. Whether he could grant it was an entirely different matter.

Helen barely registered the change of coach at The Black Swan in Holborn or the drive past Smithfield Market which was beginning to come to life with livestock and porters or the journey down the roads out of the city. The cobbled streets were left behind as the coach jogged on toward Highgate, through Hatfield and Baldock. Her fellow passengers were a constant stream of characters who boarded and left the coach for their various destinations. Some wanted to chat, some slept, most were travelling to visit family, but their visits were a distraction from her thoughts. Though Helen was desperate to meet her brother, the cost was great.

When they stopped at Stilton on the Great North Road, she penned a quick letter to her grandmother—her aunt had insisted that she would tell the dowager where she had gone and why—but Helen's experience of her aunt led her to believe that she would do nothing of the kind. She did not, however, give it to the messenger, deciding she would wait until she had actually met her brother before risking her aunt's wrath by contacting her grandmother. There was little love between the two women. They tolerated each other, and given her aunt's frame of mind, Helen believed she would actually enjoy tormenting the older woman by withholding the information.

Helen was barely aware of the towns and villages she passed, as she kept her mind occupied in her endeavor to think of anything but James. If she thought of him, she knew the tears would fall and she would not be able to stop them. That part of her life was over, and she had to accept it. She knew she must concentrate now not on what she had lost, but on what she had gained. All she could hope was that it would be worth it.

What would her brother be like; would he seem familiar at all? Her aunt had said she would send word ahead that she was coming, but what if she had not? Her own shock at learning that she had a brother would be just as much as a shock to him, learning that he had a sister. For the first time, it occurred to her that he might reject her, he might be completely happy with his foster family, and the sudden thought caused her heart to freeze. The last thing he might want could be a woman coming into his life and disrupting it. If he rejected her, she would have lost everything—James, her uncle, even her grandmother might not forgive her for running away.

As the miles rolled on, she became increasingly anxious, barely sleeping at the inns along the way and forcing herself to eat a little, though she had no appetite. The other passengers came and went, and she was happy to close her eyes and feign sleep to avoid notice and conversation. The tactic worked well until they changed at Doncaster, for by this time there were only two other passengers, an elderly married couple, and herself.

"Have you come far?" the woman asked as she settled her substantial frame opposite Helen.

"From London," she replied, hoping that would be the end of the conversation.

"Big place, London, went there once, did not like it. Yorkshire's the place for me. You can get what you need in Yorkshire and at half the price you'd pay in London," the man put in.

"Oh, George, do be quiet, the young lady does not want to listen to your opinions," the woman put in.

"Sorry, Miss. Name's Pool, George Pool, and this is my wife, Thea. Pleased to meet you, Miss...?"

"Rockingham, Helen Rockingham."

"Pardon me saying, Miss Rockingham, but it seems a little unusual for a young woman of quality such as yourself to be travelling so far on your own," Mrs. Pool ventured.

"A family emergency," Helen explained.

"Ah." The other woman nodded. "We are on our way to Edinburgh. Our daughter is about to have our first grandchild."

"How nice, congratulations," Helen responded politely.

"Of course, we have to change in York. Are you staying in York or are you travelling further?" Mr. Pool asked.

"I am travelling to Whitby to see my brother," Helen replied.

"Ah, nice place, Whitby. Good fish," Mr. Pool commented before turning over to sleep.

"Well, I hope you find your brother quite well, my dear," said Mrs. Pool.

Helen nodded. So did she.

Helen had never been to York and was disappointed to know that she would have to wait until the following day for her connection to Whitby. She could not help but be enchanted by the ancient city, which was dominated by the minster at one end and the ruins of the castle at the other. She spent the afternoon wandering through the old, narrow, cobbled streets and visiting the various markets, amazed at how close the buildings were and at the number of churches within the city walls. She had left London with very little and wanted to take a gift for her brother and also found that walking and shopping offered her a little distraction from her worries.

After what seemed like a week, she was finally able to leave the Black Swan on the final leg of her journey on the Whitby Neptune. Soon, she would at least be in the same town as her brother in a matter of hours. The other passengers consisted of a youngish man and his mother who were going to Whitby for the sea air. "For my rheumatism," the old lady explained, adding, "And why are you travelling to Whitby? Surely you do not suffer from rheumatism."

Helen smiled. Perhaps it was a Yorkshire trait, asking questions soon after meeting. "No, ma'am, I am to meet my brother, we have not seen each other in many years."

"How delightful. There is nothing like family, is there, Ashton?"

The young man looked up from the notebook in which he had been engrossed since boarding the coach. "Indeed not, Mother."

"I do not know what I should do without Ashton. He has been a tower of strength since his poor father passed away," she said, wiping a tear from her eye. "Now," she went on, her grief apparently forgotten, "where are you staying in Whitby? I know it well and can recommend the best places."

"For the moment, I shall be staying at The White Horse and Griffin on Church Street, though if my brother and I decide to stay in Whitby, I shall look for a cottage to rent." Helen stopped, quite surprised at herself for divulging her plans to a complete stranger, but she felt her spirits lifting with every mile that brought her closer to her brother. In any case, once the journey was over, there was slim chance of her ever meeting Mrs. Sutton and her son again.

"Oh, The White Horse and Griffin is quite the best inn, and we have taken a house not far, actually on Church Street itself, and if you do decide to stay and rent a cottage, I shall be more than happy to advise you of the best location. So we shall have plenty of opportunities to meet, in fact, I should like you to come to tea this afternoon."

"Mother, I rather think the young lady might want to rest and meet her brother," Ashton put in.

"Of course, you must excuse me, my dear. I rather do rattle on so. Ashton is always telling me to cease talking, as did his poor father before him."

"And she took no notice of either of us," Ashton muttered, but softened his remarks with a smile.

"Then I shall stop and leave you to your thoughts, but I shall expect you for tea before the week is out."

For the rest of the journey, mother and son talked quietly to each other and Helen was left to herself and her thoughts.

Just as they approached Whitby, the sunshine disappeared, and the town seemed to be enveloped in thick mist.

"It's a sea fret," Ashton explained, seeing Helen's alarm. "They happen at this time of year. It could be the same tomorrow, or it could have cleared this afternoon. It certainly gives the ruins an air of mystery." He gestured to the skyline where Helen could just about make out the soaring arches of buildings long gone.

"The ruins were once an abbey, but it was ruined even before Henry the Eighth ruined the rest of them. It is possible to visit, but there are one hundred and ninety-nine steps to climb in order to reach it. Though I must confess the views from the top are quite spectacular."

"Then I shall be sure to visit with my brother," Helen replied.

Helen lost sight of Ashton and his mother in the bustle of disembarkation at the inn. Servants came out to take the luggage and see to the horses, but Helen thought that once they were settled in their accommodation and she in hers, the chances were that she would not see them again.

---

*I*t had been her words that suddenly came back to him as he sat at his desk, having seen Helen safely delivered to her grandmother's house. *"I love you, whatever happens, I love you."* Once they came to the forefront of his mind, he could not forget them. They were not the words used by someone who was about to marry in a matter of hours, they were the words spoken by someone who was clearly about to do something else. His heart froze. Surely, this could not be happening again. Surely, the woman he loved was not leaving him for another, not after the night they had shared. Though, when he considered it, there had been an intensity about Helen he had not seen before, as though she knew their time together was limited. He could not shake the feeling of foreboding and called for his horse to be saddled.

As he entered the house, his fears were confirmed. Helen's grandmother sat hollow-eyed, a lace handkerchief damp from her tears. "She's gone, Tremaine. Her bed was not slept in. I do not know where she is. I came back from Hampton Court early as my friend was unwell. Otherwise, we should not have known of her disappearance for days." She dabbed her eyes again. "Do you think she could have been abducted? I know Eunice is furious at the knowledge that you and Helen are to marry, but I did not think even she would stoop so low."

James thought for a moment. "No, I do not believe Helen was abducted. I think she planned to leave, but you are right about one thing. I suspect that the Countess of Rockingham is somehow involved. She tried once before to hide Helen away."

"But Helen loves you, why would she leave without a word?"

He shook his head. "That, I do not know. Perhaps she thought she had no choice, but I intend to find out and I promise you I will bring her back. May I speak with the servants, they may have seen or heard something?"

It was the stable lad who proved to be the most helpful. He had been awake with one of the horses and seen "the lady get into a carriage before dawn." Not only that, he heard the driver tell her to hurry or she would miss the connection at the Black Swan to get to York. So she was only a few hours ahead, and if he could get messages to his agents, he could intercept her. Men on horseback would travel quicker than a young woman in a coach.

"York?" the dowager asked. "But why would Helen travel to York? She has no connections in York."

"It may be that York is not her final destination," James pondered. "In which case, it is essential that we locate her as soon as possible. Coaches from York go to all corners of the country." And beyond. Once she left York, she could be lost to him forever. "May I trouble you for pen and paper?" Within minutes, notes were dispatched, and he was on his way to see the Countess of Rockingham.

"If you expect me to tell you anything about the whereabouts of that young woman, you are sadly mistaken," the woman snapped as soon as he entered the room. Her appearance shocked James. Her usually immaculately dressed hair hung in loose grey strands and her gown was stained and crumpled.

"So, you do know where she is? Or at least where she is bound?"

"Of course I know."

"Because you arranged it?"

She smiled, but it was not pleasant. "You will never have her. I have made sure of that."

His heart almost stopped. "If she is harmed in any way…" he began.

"Oh, she is perfectly safe. I could have had her killed, it would have been simple enough, but no, she will have to live with a broken heart as I have, a much more fitting punishment."

"I do not understand." James was beginning to realize how precarious the countess's grasp on sanity had become, but he needed to keep her talking so that she might let some information slip.

"Her mother bewitched my Jonathon, he broke our engagement and married her, choosing *her*, a common miner's daughter over me. Then, when they died, to add insult to injury, Helen was forced into my family like a cuckoo in the nest. I had to bring that brat up because when they brought her from the poorhouse, my stupid husband was there. Had he been out, I would have sent her away and he would have been none the wiser. Still," she added thoughtfully, "at least he never knew about the other one."

"The babe who died?"

The countess cackled. "The babe who died, yes, the babe who died."

James thought quickly. "But the babe did not die, did it?"

The laughing stopped. "Who says so?"

"You did," James lied, his mind racing calculatingly. If this was the only way he could find out Helen's whereabouts, so be it.

Suddenly, the countess looked old and ill. "Did I?" she asked, her voice wavered. "I do not remember."

"Everyone thought the babe died, but only you knew it was alive?" he prompted.

"I sent him away and paid for him to be looked after. He's a bright boy, he goes to school. He could have been my son. My boy," she declared in an odd combination of pride and disgust.

"And you knew that Helen would not resist meeting her brother, so you gave her a choice—her own happiness with me or uniting with her only blood relative?" he suggested.

"That's right," the old woman snapped, suddenly belligerent once more. "Why should she end up a duchess one day, higher-ranked than me? Her mother was a miner's daughter, she had no right. If she married at all, she should have married whoever we saw fit."

James struggled to hold onto his patience and only managed because the woman in front of him was his only link to Helen and had unfortunately almost completely lost her wits. "You did not think that for once that Helen deserved love?"

"Love?" she screeched. "I loved Jonathon, but he did not love me, and when he broke our engagement, both our fathers decided that I would marry his brother! I did not love him, and he did not love me. Did my father care? 'You will either come to love him or not, the choice is yours,' was all he said. So do not talk to me about love! Now leave me, I am tired."

"I ask you, please, to put this right and tell me where Helen is."

She smiled slyly. "She is with her brother, far from here."

"Close to York?" he asked, hoping to provoke the old woman to give further details. His agents were on their way to catch up with the coach and following every clue as to where she was going, but he still needed as much information as he could get.

"My father took me there as a child," she said, her voice softening as her eyes closed. "Within half a day of York, the air is clean with a sea breeze, fine countryside where the cliffs are steep, the climb too…" As her features relaxed in sleep, James could see something of the handsome woman she had once been behind the harsh lines of jealousy and rage.

As he was leaving, Lord William Rockingham came through the front door. "Ah, Tremaine, good to see you. Will you take a glass of port?"

"Sadly, sir, I have no time, but I need a word about your wife."

CHAPTER 22

*H*elen consulted the piece of paper in her hand once more to check she was at the right place. She decided to come during the day when her brother should be at school, to meet the woman who had looked after him, thinking it would be easier if she could have help to introduce herself to her brother rather than shock them both. The house looked as though it had been freshly painted, the windows were spotless, and the curtains impressively white. She could see her face in the brass door knocker. Clearly, whoever was looking after her brother took pride in her home. She took a deep breath and knocked on the door. After a few moments, it was opened by a plump older woman.

"I am here to see Mrs. Harrison," she began.

"I know who yer are. Missus is expecting yer."

She followed the maid through to the parlour where a slim woman sat at a small writing desk. The room was simply but well-furnished with two comfortable chairs beside the stone fireplace. The woman was perhaps in her early forties. She stood and smiled as she held out her hand to Helen. "You must be Miss Rockingham, her ladyship sent a note that you were coming."

Helen shook her hand in silence. She had not really known what to expect, but she was surprised both at the welcome and the warmth of the woman's tone.

"Will you have some tea?" Mrs. Harrison asked when they were seated by the fire.

"Tea would be lovely, thank you." The older woman nodded to the maid, who disappeared down the corridor.

"Mrs. Harrison," Helen began.

"Please call me Ruby, we do not stand on ceremony here, Miss Rockingham."

Helen had come prepared to dislike this woman, but found herself instantly liking her, replying, "In which case, please call me Helen." She smiled.

"I am sure her ladyship explained why I am here."

"You are Johnny's long-lost sister, but I would have known that instantly."

It was with shock that Helen realized she had been so intent on the journey and getting to see him that she had not thought to ask his name.

"Johnny?"

"Her ladyship named him Jonathon, for his father, I believe," Ruby explained.

"And you have looked after him since?"

"Since he was brought here as a babe. Such a little thing he was, to be honest we did not think he would survive—and had he been left in that place, he would not have."

"I do not understand, how did he come to live here? Rockingham is many miles away, near to Richmond."

"My late sister was one of the wardens of the Workhouse, the one that took you to your aunt and uncle..." Ruby hesitated.

"Please go on," Helen prompted. "I want to know everything, even though some of it might be difficult to hear."

"Ada, my sister, could be a hard woman at times, but underneath she had a heart of gold. To be honest, Helen, she did not take to your aunt at all. She found her to be a cold, unfeeling woman. She thought she was giving you the chance of a better life with your rich relatives."

"Then why did she not bring my brother to live with me?"

"Having seen your aunt's coldness, Ada was ready to take you away again, but your uncle insisted you stay and be raised a lady. She decided quickly that your brother would be better off in a more lowly family where he might not have wealth, but he would be loved. So she told the countess that the babe was sickly and likely to die within the week. Fortunately, he became well, and Ada saw to it that he began to thrive."

They were interrupted by the maid arriving with the tea. They sat silently as she set it up between them. When they were again alone, Helen asked, "So how did Johnny come to you?"

Ruby smiled at the memory. "My sister knew that Captain Harrison and I were desperate to have a child, but I am unable to carry a babe to full term, so when she told us she had a baby who needed a home, we were delighted to take him in."

Helen took a sip of tea. "And all of this so far happened without my aunt's knowledge?"

Ruby's smile slipped. "A month after you were left with your aunt and uncle, her ladyship visited the poorhouse. When one of the wardens told her the baby had survived and that Ada had taken him for adoption, she summoned Ada and threatened her with dismissal if she did not immediately tell her where the baby was. My poor sister had little in her life beyond her work at that place. Anyway, her ladyship came to this house several days later."

"Did she threaten to take Johnny away?"

Ruby shook her head. "Quite the opposite. She wanted to ensure that he would be brought up with a degree of comfort, indeed, she has always been both generous and prompt in paying toward his keep. At that time, we were thinking of calling him Henry, after my husband, but her ladyship insisted we call him Jonathon."

Helen considered that for a moment. She had thought there was nothing in her aunt but hatred for her parents, but this seemed like a sure sign that Eunice still had some love for her first fiancé. Naming him for his father was a good sign, she was sure.

"Did she make other visits?"

"No, that was the only time she came, but she demanded that we send her regular reports of his progress and there is money to send him to university if that is his desire when the time comes. She has sent more than sufficient money to ensure that Johnny has wanted for nothing. Indeed, when my husband was lost at sea, she increased her payments."

"I am sorry to hear of your loss."

Ruby looked at the portrait above the mantelpiece wistfully. "Henry was a good man, and it was a long time ago, but I still miss him. The countess sent a letter of condolence."

Helen shook her head. "The more I hear of my aunt, the less I understand her."

Ruby looked at her for a moment before replying, "It is my opinion that in some respects, Johnny is the son she never had, but for some reason best known to herself, she could not bring herself to accept him fully. She did not wish him harm; indeed, she seems to have wanted him to have success in life, but she could never personally be involved in his life. As I say, it is only my opinion."

"And does Johnny know anything about his family?" Helen asked.

"Not until a few days ago when a message came to say that you would be arriving. I was to tell him of his sister, but that you would tell him the rest."

"And how did he take the news that he has other family?"

Ruby considered the question for a moment. "My husband and I agreed when we took Johnny in as a baby that, regardless of your aunt's instruction, he should know he is not our natural child, so he knew there was a family somewhere. He is looking forward to meeting you." She smiled. "In fact, as soon as he sees you and you see him, you would instantly have recognized each other as brother and sister."

They were interrupted by the clattering of the front door. "That will be Johnny now."

---

*R*uby was right, she would have known him anywhere. He had her chestnut hair and the same deep blue eyes, though she could also see their father when she thought of the miniature James had given her. At thirteen, he was almost as tall as she.

"Hello, you must be Johnny." She smiled and held out her hand, not quite knowing what his response would be.

The boy smiled shyly. "And you are Helen, my sister." He bowed and shook her hand.

There was a silence before she said, "You must feel it strange, suddenly finding you have a sister."

"A little," he agreed. "But in a nice way," he added.

The silence was broken by the maid bustling in with more tea, muffins, and cakes to which Johnny helped himself. "Johnny is always ravenous when he returns from school," Ruby explained, laughing as he reached for a second muffin.

"So, how do you like school?" Helen asked.

"I like mathematics and science, history, and geography too. Latin and Greek are all right."

"Johnny used to attend the grammar school, but we moved him to Dawson's Academy where the curriculum is wider. As well as Latin and Greek, he speaks French, German, and a little Italian," Ruby explained proudly.

"My, that is most impressive," Helen declared. "At my school, we wasted much time on flower arranging and dancing. I am afraid girls were not encouraged to learn a great deal."

"I should like to be an engineer or a sea captain, like my Uncle Henry."

Helen's eyes filled with tears. "Both your father and grandfather were engineers."

"Why don't you take Helen for a walk to the abbey ruins, Johnny, now that you have finished your tea?" Ruby suggested. "I am sure there is much you want to ask her and there will be much she wants to know about you."

Helen looked gratefully at the older woman, knowing it would be easier for her to speak to her brother alone.

As the front door closed behind them, Johnny turned to her. "Are you intending to take me away from Aunt Ruby?"

"Are you afraid of that?" she asked, her heart lurching.

"I do not want to leave her. Since Uncle Henry died, I am the man of the house."

Helen thought for a moment. She had been naïve, selfish even, to imagine that she could waltz into Johnny's life and that he would fall in with her plans without protest. Of course he would want to stay with the woman who had been the only mother he had known. He was happy with her, why would he want to leave?

"Then how about I take a house here in Whitby so that we may see each other as often as you wish?" she suggested. "And if you wanted to, sometimes you might come and stay with me."

"I think I should like that."

"Then it's settled, I shall start to look for a house tomorrow." This was what she had planned for, though in her imagination she and her brother would be there together. But she must be content with what she had. A week ago, she had not known she even had a brother. A week ago, she should have been married to James.

"Now, let's go to the abbey, there are one-hundred and ninety-nine steps. My friends and I have races, but as you are a girl, I doubt you would want to," Johnny's voice broke into her thoughts.

"What makes you so sure?"

"It's just not the sort of thing girls do," he explained.

"Then be prepared to be beaten." Without further ado, Helen picked up her skirts and began to run up the steps. It took Johnny a second or two to realize, and then he sprinted after her. They reached the top together, laughing and panting as they both caught their breath.

"I would have beaten you easily if you had played fair," Johnny grumbled good-naturedly.

"Ah, a useful lesson in life, Johnny. Girls sometimes have to be unfair in order to ensure that life is fairer for them," she replied, adjusting her bonnet.

"I do not understand."

"Well, as an educated young man, you will have the opportunity to travel, earn your living, and more or less do as you choose. It is rather different for girls."

Johnny shook his head. "I still do not understand. Girls are to be protected, they are delicate."

"Girls are not brought up to be independent, they must depend on their fathers or husbands for money and security."

"Do you have a husband?"

The question came so suddenly that Helen had to turn her head to hide the tears that sprang to her eyes. "No," she said quietly. "No, I do not have a husband. Now," she went on brightly, "let us explore the ruins."

CHAPTER 23

$\mathcal{H}$elen's days settled into a pattern. She spent the morning at the inn writing, looking at potential properties she might rent until she could afford to buy, and dealing with the correspondence from her publisher who had released the book in London. Mr. Thompson was very pleased with the reviews and was planning to print and distribute more within weeks. He expected that there would be copies of her book in every town and city in the country by the year's end. He was most eager to know about the progress of her next book.

In the afternoons, she visited Ruby, who was fast becoming a good friend, and who introduced her to other women in the town. When Johnny came home from school, the two of them usually went for a walk along the cliff top or the beach if the tide was out. They spent the evenings reading and playing games before she returned to her rooms at the hotel.

One afternoon, after she had been in Whitby for almost a month, Ruby said, "I think when you are settled in your own home, Johnny should live with you."

Ruby raised her eyes to her husband's portrait for a moment before continuing, "Your coming here was a godsend, my dear. I did not know what to do, but now that you are here I can go, knowing that Johnny will be loved and looked after when I am gone."

"What do you mean?" Helen was alarmed.

"I am dying, Helen. My heart has never been strong since I had a fever as a child. It is probably the reason the captain and I could never have children of our own."

"Oh no, please, Ruby, do not speak like this."

Ruby smiled. "We must be practical, and the doctor says my heart is weak and failing. As a matter of fact, he said it was a miracle I have gone on for so long. But each day, it gets a little harder. I need you to be strong, for me and for Johnny."

"I understand."

"And if you want to, you can live in this little house if it suits your needs. It will be Johnny's in any case, and it might be for the best if he is not disrupted, at least until he finishes his education."

"Of course," Helen agreed. "How much does Johnny know?" she asked.

"He knows I struggle, but I have kept the severity of my condition from him." She took a sip of tea. "Your appearance here, my dear, is the answer to my prayers. I shall be able to die comfortably knowing that there is someone to take care of Johnny."

Helen took the older woman's hand. "I promise I will look after Johnny and make sure he never forgets you."

The two women embraced and tried to smile through their tears. "I shall tell Johnny tonight," Ruby promised.

The following afternoon, Johnny was quiet as he and Helen walked along the beach.

Helen decided that it was best to face the issue head-on rather than allow Johnny to brood over it. "I believe Ruby must have spoken to you last night," she began.

Johnny nodded. "Is it true?" he asked.

"I believe so," she replied.

"Ruby says that I may live with you when…when the time comes."

Helen nodded.

"I should like that." He smiled, but there was no hiding the sadness in his eyes.

"Ruby has left the cottage to you, so nothing needs to change," Helen reassured him.

"But everything will change! Aunt Ruby will not be there!" he cried, for the first time seeming like the child he was rather than a young man.

"No," Helen agreed. "I wish it were otherwise, but there are some things we have no control over." Unbidden, an image of James flashed into her mind. "Even when the worst things happen, we manage to cope, because we have to. What we should do now," she added briskly, "is ensure that we make the most of the time we have left with Ruby."

Johnny nodded solemnly.

It seemed that once Ruby was satisfied that Johnny had someone to look after him, she could die in peace. Within a month, Helen and Johnny were walking up the hundred-and-ninety-nine steps to the graveyard at the top of the cliff. Helen carried lilies, Ruby's favourite flower, to place on the grave. Ruby had been most insistent that there be no elaborate mourning rituals and banned both of them from excessive wearing of black, declaring that it should be reserved for the funeral only and that they should celebrate her life as she had, grateful to have married her beloved captain and raised a wonderful son.

In the end, Helen had opted for a grey gown and pelisse while Johnny wore a black armband. When they had finished laying the flowers, Helen said, "I think I shall go for a short walk on the beach." She had not known Ruby long but mourned her connection to this new life and her new brother.

"I will walk down with you, but I have some Latin to finish. Will you be all right on your own?"

Helen smiled. "Of course." Since Ruby's death, Johnny had taken his duties as man of the house very seriously. "Perhaps when you have finished, you might join me. I do not think there will be many people walking, so you should find me."

"Just be aware of the tide and do not go too far, there's a sea fret coming."

"Spoken like the son of a sea captain," Helen said and laughed. "But I shall take care," she assured him gently.

Johnny was right, the light clouds had begun to obscure the weak sun and the waves crashed on the shore dragging sand and pebbles back and forth and far out to sea as the mist had begun to rise. Helen strode along the waterline, reflecting on the changes in her life that the last few weeks of her life had brought. She would never forget her joy at finding her brother and the welcome and warmth she had received from Ruby, but she felt empty. Although she filled her days as much as she could, James was never far from her thoughts. She knew he would never forgive her, so she was grateful that she had the memory of their one night together as it would have to last her a lifetime. If she could not have James, she knew that no other man would do. She had even hoped that a child might have resulted from their night together, a child of his that she would have raised in love, but even that was not to be.

She sat on a large boulder at the foot of the cliff which had probably been thrown there by the sea lifetimes ago, and she wept. She wept for Ruby's life, cut off too soon, for her parents, who did not live to see their children, and for herself. She did not usually allow herself to indulge in tears, but for once her control slipped. After so long yearning for happiness and abiding mistreatment in the dark, why, when happiness had finally seemed within her grasp, had it been snatched away? Why could she not have both the only man she would ever love and her brother as well? Why was her life a collection of cruel choices?

When her tears eased, she took out her handkerchief and blew her nose. Her life would not be perfect, no one's was, and she had no entitlement to be happy all the time, no one did. What she must do, she determined, was to ensure that she savoured the happiness that had come into her life. She had her career as a writer, she had her brother, she now had enough money to live comfortably, and a roof over her head. She had much for which to be thankful. She just hoped that the hole in her heart James had left would one day heal and give her peace. She had at least known love, and that was something many girls of any class could not say.

*I*t would be best for Johnny to maintain his routine, Helen decided, as they both adjusted to life without Ruby. She remembered how she had felt losing first one parent and then the other, and her brother had now lost the two people who had raised him and loved him as though he were their own son. Helen was grateful that Betty, Ruby's maid, and the cook had both decided to come into her employ and remain with the household, so all continued to run as it had before.

Each morning, Johnny left for school shortly after breakfast and returned in the afternoon. If the weather was fine, he and Helen took a walk on the beach, or along the cliffs. Every Sunday Jonathon placed a posy of flowers on Ruby's grave. Sometimes, Helen visited it on her own, for though Ruby had been in her life for such a short time, she felt her loss deeply.

While Johnny was at school, Helen concentrated on her writing, finding comfort in creating happier lives for others when her own life was filled with a degree of sadness and uncertainty. She had worried that she would not have sufficient funds to support the little household, but the money sent by Mr. Thompson and the bank drafts from her aunt were more than enough to cover their needs.

As she became a familiar figure in the town, she began to make the acquaintance of some of the local society, and soon the women of Whitby's gentry began to call, initially to offer their condolences. The first to call was Mrs. Wraithe, wife of the vicar. Ruby had been a well-liked and respected woman and would be sorely missed. "Perhaps," she suggested, "Miss Rockingham would consider joining the Charitable Society for the Relief of the Poor. A position previously held by Mrs. Harrison?" Helen sensed, when this invitation was extended, that she had passed some sort of test and was accepted into Whitby's society.

Within weeks, Helen was fully immersed into the life in Whitby. If this was to be her home now, she reasoned, then she must make a life for herself. It might also help her to put her hopes and dreams of the life she might have had with James behind her. She knew she could never forget him, how could she? A love like that would come only once in a lifetime, even if one was fortunate. She would always treasure the memory of their all too brief romance and she hoped that, in time, she would be able to consider the memories of their time together with less pain. Perhaps one day the black desolation she felt when she thought of what might have been would recede, but even several weeks after leaving London, she still had days when she battled a melancholy that threatened to overwhelm her. Fortunately, Jonathon seemed unaware of her dark mood when it appeared, and she was careful to pin a bright smile on her face whenever he was present. He had lost a much-loved parent, his loss was far greater, and it was her duty to help him get over it as best she could.

"There is to be a dance at the Assembly Rooms," Mrs. Wraithe announced on one of her visits. "Just a small affair, in aid of the Poor Society. It is time you fully rejoined society, Miss Rockingham, if I may say so."

Helen put down her cup. "I do not think it is appropriate, Mrs. Wraithe. After all, I am still in mourning."

"Stuff and nonsense. Ruby was an eminently sensible woman and would not want you locking yourself away like a nun. You must attend, everyone will be there. It will be the perfect opportunity to announce your full debut into local society."

Helen smiled. "Mrs. Wraithe, I thank you for your concern, truly I do, but quite apart from anything else, I have no chaperone."

"The Reverend will escort us both and I shall act as your chaperone. This is not London, or even York. Rules are not so strict here. Besides," she continued, taking the last lemon tart, "if being escorted by the vicar and chaperoned by the vicar's wife is not respectable enough, I do not know what is," she finished, and smartly popped the lemon tart into her mouth.

Helen considered her situation. It would seem that Mrs. Wraithe was determined to launch her into Whitby society and any objections would be quickly dispensed with. "Very well," she heard herself saying. "Thank you for your kind invitation. I shall be delighted to accompany you."

The following Saturday, Helen sat looking at her reflection in the cheval mirror. Without a lady's maid, she had learned to put up her own hair in a simple Grecian knot. It was not one of the more elaborate styles she had worn in London, but there again, Whitby was not London. She had chosen a pale lilac gown, the most elaborate of the gowns she had brought with her. A band of pansies embroidered at the waist and hem relieved its stark simplicity. As always, she wore the gold locket with her father's portrait. Pinning a matching bunch of embroidered pansies in her hair, she gave herself a final look before picking up her shawl and reticule. She would do.

The dance was already in full swing when she arrived with the Wraithes. The Assembly Room was not large, most people seemed to know each other, and they certainly all seemed to know the Wraithes as they made their way through the throng.

"Ah, Miss Rockingham, I was hoping you would attend," came a voice through the crowd. Helen looked up and saw Mrs. Sutton, followed by her son, bearing down on her. "I see you have quite settled in Whitby," the older woman declared. "We, too, have decided to stay for a while. I find the air most efficacious. Ashton," she added, tapping her son sharply on the arm with her fan, "you remember Miss Rockingham from our journey?"

"Yes, Mother."

"I rather expected to see more of you, Miss Rockingham, but I assume you have been busy with family matters. That is why you came, is it not?"

"You are correct, ma'am." Mrs. Sutton was one of those women who, given half a chance, would have one's life story within half an hour of meeting. "Unfortunately, we suffered a bereavement shortly after I arrived, which rather took my brother and I by surprise," she explained.

"My condolences," Mrs. Sutton replied before quickly saying, "Ashton, what are you thinking? Ask Miss Rockingham to dance. Don't just stand there like a dolt."

"Miss Rockingham, would you…"

"Of course," Helen interrupted him, anxious to avoid Mrs. Sutton's inquisitiveness.

"You must not mind Mother," Ashton explained. "She is just very interested in people." Helen smiled in reply as he swept her onto the dance floor. He was surprisingly strong for one so dominated by his mother, and taller than she had first thought.

"So, Miss Rockingham, do you intend to make Whitby your home? It is a fine town."

"For the time being, as my brother is still young and has many friends here. When he is a little older, we shall have to see."

"Do you wish to travel? Some women are doing that now, I believe."

Helen thought for a moment as they turned, before murmuring, "I should like to see the pyramids of Egypt and lions in Africa, though I doubt I shall."

"Ah, you would like to see the lions hunt."

For a second, Helen was taken back to her first dance with James when she had laughingly told him lionesses do the hunting. She smiled sadly. "For the moment I am content to be in Whitby."

For the remainder of the dance, Ashton kept her entertained with snippets of gossip about the local gentry his mother had gleaned. When their waltz was over, he escorted her back to her party and returned with a glass of lemonade and for the rest of the evening was never far from her side.

"Well, my dear," Mrs. Wraithe said as the settled into the carriage for the journey home, "you certainly seem to have been a success with one young and, may I say, eligible man this evening."

Helen laughed at her friend's obvious matchmaking. "Mr. Sutton and I danced one waltz and chatted a little, that is all." She had enjoyed his easy and pleasant manner, but he didn't make her feel like James had and she had no reason to think that might change. Ashton seemed like a sweet man, but he didn't have the fire within him that James had so readily.

"Ashton Sutton is quite the catch of the season here in Whitby. His great-grandfather was a wealthy farmer, and his grandfather started Sutton's Bank, I believe," Mrs. Wraithe went on. "I had a long conversation with his dear mother, who is very keen to see him settled."

"I am sure Mr. Sutton is indeed a fine young man, but I am really not at all interested in marriage. I have my brother to look after," Helen replied firmly, hoping she had nipped Mrs. Wraithe's matchmaking in the bud.

"Is there a sweetheart you have left behind? In London perhaps?" the older woman persisted.

There was no point in lying, and she took a deep breath before replying, "There was someone with whom I had an attachment, but it was not..." Helen clamped her lips together before her voice could break, even saying so little had brought back painful memories.

"I am so sorry, my dear." Mrs. Wraithe placed a comforting hand on Helen's arm. "Broken hearts do mend, eventually."

"I am sure they do," Helen spoke quietly. But she was also sure that it could happen only once, and they always bear the scar.

Helen paused before she opened the door and dashed a tear from her cheek, angry at herself for not being able to accept her new life, even after months of effort. Would she never be able to think of James without this feeling of desolation?

CHAPTER 24

The door opened suddenly, startling her out of her thoughts. "You have a visitor," Betty announced with a gleam in her eye. "From London. In the front parlour." She took Helen's shawl and almost ran down the corridor to open the door. As she walked down the corridor patting her hair in place, Helen racked her brains to think who might be calling from London and at this time of night. The only communication she had had was with Mr. Thompson, but she had made it absolutely clear that he was in no way to share her address with anyone, not even her grandmother. As much as it agonized her, she had done as her aunt demanded and told no one where she was, not even her grandmother, fearful of her aunt's malice. She worried not only about what her aunt might do to her and Johnny, but how she might punish or harm her grandmother. The countess had never been a kind woman and at their last meeting had seemed quite deranged at times, there was no accounting for how her mind was working or what actions she might take.

She had seen nothing of the news in London since she left, she could not bear to read of James attending balls and dancing with other women. In fact, she tried not to think of London at all, though she wondered from time to time what reason her aunt had conjured up to explain her sudden departure. "Miss Helen is here," Betty announced as Helen stepped through the door.

The sight that met her when she entered her room cleared her mind so thoroughly that she stared blankly, not able to comprehend what was before her...James and Johnny sat at the table, their heads together. "Ah," James said, looking up with a smile, "the trials of algebra, I remember it well from my school days." He seemed comfortable, as though his appearance in the small parlour was a regular occurrence.

"Helen, this is His Lord Tremaine, Marquess of Woodville," Johnny solemnly introduced them, his slight mistake bringing the twitch of a smile to her lips, "though he says you are already acquainted."

"Yes, I...er...yes...we..." Helen stammered before gathering her scattered thoughts. "Johnny, I am quite at a loss to know why you are not in bed, but perhaps you could go and ask for some tea."

Johnny looked sheepish. "I am sorry, Helen, I had a bad dream and could not get back to sleep, so I came down for some warm milk like I used to do with Aunt Ruby. I noticed the light under the door and came in and met Lord Tremaine."

"Johnny, dear, Lord Tremaine and I must speak privately. No need to worry," she added, cutting off his protest. "Betty will be just beyond the door to chaperone, so we need not your services. Off to bed with you." She smiled reassuringly.

For several moments after he left, all that could be heard were the ticking of the clock and the occasional crackle of the fire. Helen looked at her feet, not knowing what to say, almost not believing that James was actually in the room.

James did not take his eyes off her, using all his willpower to not walk the two strides across the room and take her in his arms. They had been apart for only a few weeks, but it felt like a lifetime. She was a little thinner than when they had parted, her violet eyes looked huge in her delicate face, and she looked as though she had been recently crying. If he had his way, she would never have to cry again.

When he had discovered her aunt's plans, it had not taken long for him to dispatch riders to find out exactly where Helen was, sending agents to pose as couples along her journey. He had known where Helen was coming and why almost as soon as she had. It had been his first thought to follow her at once, but he held back. If Helen was to have any kind of relationship with her newly found brother, he knew that he needed to give them some time to get used to the idea and get to know each other. Having met Johnny, he could see much of Helen in him. Ruby and the sea captain had done a fine job of raising him.

"My lord," he heard Helen's soft contralto voice say, "you cannot stay. If my aunt finds out we have met, she will take Johnny from me. I know it, and I know that she will ensure we never see each other again." Her voice shook as she went on. "I vowed never to contact you and I will not break it for his detriment."

He was by her side in two steps, his arms went around her, and he pulled her close, breathing in the scent of lemon and roses before she could even think to hesitate. "Helen, my dearest Helen, nothing will ever separate us again," he whispered harshly as he bent his head and found her lips in a long, drugging kiss, holding onto her tightly so that she could not break away. He put all the love he felt into that kiss, drinking her in like a man who had wandered through a desert for the last few weeks and had now found the lushest, richest oasis in the kingdom.

He broke the kiss and took a step back, still holding her. "I think you and I must talk now," he said breathlessly, leading her to the sofa and sitting beside her, holding both her small hands in his as though to give her strength. "First, you must tell me your story and then I shall tell you how I came here."

"And then you will leave?" He could still hear the fear in her voice.

"If that is what you wish," he replied, having arrived with no intention of leaving her ever again, but he instinctively knew that she could not relax with the thought of the long reach of her venomous aunt still a threat. If she still insisted he leave, for love of her, he would do so.

Once she started, the story came tumbling out—the meeting with her aunt, the shock that the baby she thought had died was in fact still alive and well, the promise that her aunt extracted to disappear without warning and abandon those who loved her, how she had travelled alone and made friends with Ruby who had since died, and how she planned to stay with Johnny in Whitby, at least until he finished his schooling.

James listened in silence as Helen explained, "My aunt, you see, blamed my mother for stealing my father away from her. She could not punish my mother, so she transferred her anger toward me and when she had the opportunity to deny me the man I loved as she had been denied hers, she took it." Helen took a breath. "That is the reason why you must leave, my lord. I am sure that should my aunt find that you have been here, she will find some way to punish me further by taking Johnny away from me forever."

She made to rise, but James pulled her firmly back. "Let me tell you of how I came here," he said, kissing the backs of her hands, and sending shivers down her back that she barely managed to repress.

"I knew you would not have given yourself to me that night then willingly disappear to elope with someone else. I knew there had to be a reason, and I remembered your words 'whatever happens,' which alarmed me when I had time to think on them. I went to your grandmother's house and found her distraught."

"Poor Grandmama," Helen murmured. "I did not wish to cause her pain."

"Your grandmama is perfectly fine," he assured her, "more of her in a moment. Some instinct told me that the countess was involved, and I went straight to see her. She was in a sorry state, perhaps all those years of hatred, plotting and planning revenge on your mother had taken their toll, but she was not in her right mind. Again, I will tell you more of her shortly.

"I managed to glean information from your aunt and various servants to work out where you were going and sent riders to shadow you on your journey. I had to be sure you were safe."

"I met some delightful people who made sure I was not alone at the inns," Helen put in.

"I know, they were some of my people who had strict instructions to ensure that you arrived safely, but without being intrusive. The hardest thing was not tearing after you myself, but I knew I had to wait until you had met your brother and you were both used to the idea of each other."

"You knew where I was all along?" Helen asked incredulously.

He nodded.

She thought for a moment. James was right. She and Johnny had needed time to get to know each other and begin to make their relationship. "Thank you," she said simply. "I shall never forget what you have done."

James was still not at ease. Since the beginning of their conversation, Helen had become controlled to the point of near rigidity. She was planning to send him away and he could not let it come to that. He had almost lost her, and he had no intention of leaving this room until she had once again consented to be his wife. "You have nothing more to fear from your aunt, my lady," he said quietly. "She will never be able to hurt you again."

Helen's eyes widened. "Why? Is she...?"

He smiled. "No, she is not dead, but she is very sick and increasingly frail and has completely lost her senses. It is as though she has forgotten much of her life. She does not recognize your uncle or her daughter and believes she is a young girl again. The earl has taken her to a clinic in Switzerland where the doctor specializes in treating maladies of the mind."

"Will he be able to cure her?"

He shook his head. "There is no cure for a malady like this. Your aunt will be treated well, but she will gradually fade away. The only kind thing that can be said about this disease is that your aunt has no knowledge of what she has become."

"But what of my uncle?"

"He will stay with her until the end and then I believe he intends to stay on the continent. He has no intention of returning to England, but I shall tell you more of that shortly."

"But why?"

"That part entails what is to happen to young Jonathon."

CHAPTER 25

*H*elen took a sip of her tea the next afternoon and watched as James and Johnny chatted easily. James was regaling Johnny with tales of his own schooldays and Johnny was laughing. She noted that Johnny was entirely comfortable with James. Perhaps he had missed the company of a man since the captain's death. Finally, James put down his teacup. "There is a matter of some importance I need to discuss with you."

"Of course, sir." Johnny made to leave.

James held up his hand quickly. "You need to stay, this concerns both you and your sister. Helen knows part of the story, but there have been recent developments that will affect both your lives,"—he paused —"and possibly mine as well."

"Go on," Helen urged, puzzled.

James took a breath. "Helen, you may remember when I investigated your family a little while ago and found that, although your grandfather, the previous earl, had threatened to disinherit your father, he did not enact it in law?"

Helen nodded.

"This means, in effect, your uncle was never the rightful earl." He turned to Johnny. "You, young man, are in fact the rightful earl, as the only legitimate son of your father."

"I do not understand," Johnny stammered.

"You were, sadly, born after your father's death, but he was legally married to your mother and that makes you the legitimate heir to the earldom. You are lawfully Jonathon Thomas William Rockingham, fifth Earl of Rockingham. You are, in fact, a very wealthy young man. Your uncle has managed your estates well."

"But what of my uncle? Will he not contest this? After all, he has lived as earl for many years," Helen asked.

James shook his head. "I discussed this with him before he left to be with his wife in the sanitorium. Your uncle is only too happy to abdicate the title. He said he never felt comfortable with it and argued with his father about Jonathon's disinheritance. He had no idea that his father had not followed through on his threat. He is happy to revert to being The Honorable Mr. Rockingham."

"I doubt Aunt Eunice would be so happy."

"Your aunt is no longer in a place where she is aware of her status. It matters not to her now whether she is Lady Eunice or The Honorable Mrs. Rockingham, she does not know. Your uncle, as I mentioned, is more than happy to remain on the continent. He believes it will help the matter to settle quicker if he does not appear in London society."

"And Clarice?" Helen asked.

"Clarice rejected the Earl of Prescot and is about to marry a rich banker twice her age. I do not think you need to worry about her, she will not lack comfort or security." James chuckled.

"I feel sorry for all of them," Helen said thoughtfully. "Aunt Eunice would hate the fact that she is no longer in control and poor Uncle always felt he was second best both as a son and a husband. And Clarice knew she could never be the son they wanted."

James could not help but smile, in love with how Helen always thought of the feelings of others. "When I spoke to your uncle, he was quite content to stay with your aunt until the end. Despite all, he has grown to love her. Then he intends to travel extensively on the continent, taking up the art he was never allowed to practice by his father. He is even thinking of travelling to the Americas, fascinated by the land and its people. In all honesty, I believe he now feels liberated to live his life the way he has always wanted to live it, free from the responsibilities he never wanted. He did, however, ask your forgiveness and wishes you to know that he never intended to be a usurper."

"Of course not," Helen replied. "No one would ever think that of him. We are all victims of a singular set of circumstances."

"But how can I be an earl?" Johnny asked, incredulous. "I have lived all my life in Whitby, I have no knowledge of what I must do as an earl."

Helen put her arm around his shoulders. "For the moment, all you need to do is finish your education here and then at university, then you might travel for a year or so. Many men do not come into their inheritance until they are much older than you. There is plenty of time to learn and there will be many people to help you."

"Of course," James added. "My own brother and I were not brought up with any expectation of land or title, yet we both had to learn. You are a bright lad, so can you."

"Will you help me, Lord Tremaine?"

"I am sure Lord Tremaine will be too busy with his own estates, but perhaps he will be able to recommend a good manager who you can trust," Helen interrupted quickly, not wanting Johnny to get too hopeful or disappointed.

James was puzzled by Helen's quick interjection. Why would he not be willing to help his young brother-in-law to be, and why was Helen addressing him formally again? "If that is what you want," he told young Jonathon.

"Will I have to move to London? Where shall I live? This house"—he looked around himself helplessly—"has always been my home."

"If you wish to remain here, then you may, of course, but I cannot pretend that your life will not change. As Earl of Rockingham, you have Rockingham Castle, a large manor house in the country, a London house, and a smaller estate in Scotland. Being an earl means great privilege but brings great responsibility. You will have many people working for you who owe their livelihoods to you. As a responsible landowner, it means that you cannot neglect the land or its people," James said very seriously. "There are bad landowners who take from the land as selfish parasites, living off their tenants' and workers' efforts who do as little as they can, doing nothing to deserve the riches they have been given."

"I understand responsibility, sir, and shall do my best to ensure I live up to the task."

Helen could have wept at the sight of the two people she loved most in the world in complete agreement. Were more landowners as socially aware of the needs of the people in their care, there would be no need for the horrors of the Workhouse.

"I would like to go to bed now, I have much to think about." Johnny stood and held his hand out to James. "Thank you, sir. When I awoke this morning, I was an ordinary boy. I hope I may look to you for guidance."

Helen suddenly felt uncomfortable once Johnny left the two of them alone. James filled the sitting room making it feel small, and she shifted awkwardly. He had come to find her and had delivered news of Johnny's inheritance in a kind manner, neither patronizing, nor sensationalizing the news. It seemed like a lifetime ago that James told her that her father had not in fact been disinherited, but at the time she had not known she had a living sibling, let alone a brother for whom the information was life-changing. His life from now on would be very different, as would hers. With all that had happened in the last few months—leaving her home and family forever, finding her brother, and Ruby's death—she had not given the matter any thought at all, leaving the Rockingham estate secret with her past.

James watched her closely, wondering what thoughts were behind the expressions flashing across her lovely face. He found himself holding his breath when she spoke.

"Thank you, Lord Tremaine, for your kindness in taking the time and trouble to come and tell us about Johnny's inheritance," she said as she stood. "I am sure, now you have delivered the news, you must be anxious to be on your way." She held out her hand, barely suppressing her shaking. If he did not leave immediately, she would surely collapse into tears in front of him and she could not bear the thought of it. Since the death of her mother, she had learned to cry alone, where no one would witness her pain. She knew, once James left, that Johnny would need to go to London and take his place as Earl of Rockingham. She would have to accustom herself to seeing James without wanting to be in his arms, because she would inevitably run into him in London from time to time. Johnny would have obligations in town, and until he had a wife, it would be her duty as his sister to accompany him.

James strode toward the door, but instead of opening it, he turned the key and put it in his pocket. "If I thought for one moment that you really wanted me to leave, I would, but your eyes tell me a different story. Tell me you do not love me, that there is nothing between us, and I will go. But tell me the truth, you owe me that."

"I..." Helen hesitated. It was enough for him. He was instantly at her side and she found herself in his arms, his fingers threaded through her hair, and her mouth covered in kisses. He gave her but a moment to breathe before dropping kisses on her eyelids and down her throat and up again to whisper fiercely in her ear, "Tell me now, Helen, tell me how you feel when I do this, tell me you have no desire for me to make love to you, tell me you do not love me, and I will walk out of the door."

"I...I cannot," she whispered. "I cannot tell you I do not love you, James, you know I do. But I left you, I abandoned you. How can you possibly forgive me?"

"There is nothing to forgive, darling. You did what you had to do in the circumstances, anyone would have done the same."

"I never stopped loving you, James, I swear, all the time I could never stop loving you."

He stepped back, still keeping his arms around her so that he could see into her magnificent eyes. "Thank God," he said emphatically. "You have no idea how much I feared you might have changed your mind while we have been apart. I have not slept well since you left, my brother almost banned me from his house due to my bad temper. I even managed to upset my sister-in-law and she is the most patient person I know. My secretary threatened to resign. If you do not promise—right now—to marry me as soon as possible, I swear I shall have no friends, no servants, and no business." He smiled. He looked in her eyes and said seriously, "I mean it, Helen. I want you in every way it is possible for a man to want a woman—in my bed, by my side, at the centre of my hearth and home, but mostly here." He took her hand and placed it on his chest. "Here, in my heart."

Tears filled her eyes. "Oh, James, I do love you, I always have, you saw something in me I could not see for myself—that I was worthy of love. These last few weeks have been so hard, I wanted to explain why I had to go away and yet I could not because I was afraid my aunt would find some way to take Johnny away. I was so terrified that you would quickly forget me. I dreaded finding out you had found another woman, one more suitable than me. All I could do was remember our night together. I am sure you found me forward, but I knew that if I was to leave you forever, I needed to have one memory that could never be taken from me."

His eyes glowed. "I too could not forget that night, nor would I ever want to. And I will ensure that your life is full of many, many more wonderful nights"

CHAPTER 26

*J*ames could not take his eyes from his bride as she walked slowly toward him on the arm of her brother, the young Earl of Rockingham. He felt his eyes moisten and he knew he would always remember her in this moment, radiant as a bride should be, for the rest of his life.

"She is certainly a beauty, your Miss Nobody," his brother murmured, patting his arm. "If our brides were ever to become aware of the power they have over us, we should be completely and utterly lost."

"I am quite sure Helen has an idea, as does Emily, no doubt. It is just that they graciously allow us to imagine it is the other way around." James grinned.

"Ah, beauty and brains, both of them," Robert replied. "A heady combination."

"Heady indeed," James agreed, smiling warmly as his bride reached his side.

"Dearly beloved…" the vicar began.

Helen had been shaking as she walked down the aisle, but her nerves calmed the moment James smiled at her. The day had begun with her grandmother sitting next to her bed as she nibbled a piece of toast which her grandmother had insisted on, saying, "You need something inside you, a wedding day is a very long day, especially for a bride." Then, sensing Helen's nervousness, she had regaled her with the tale of how one of her friends married her husband only because her father held a sword to his back, and yet "still, they had five sons, so something must have worked out."

After breakfast, she had bathed and dressed in a robe while her hair was dried, and she dressed it with white Stephanotis flowers from the Duke of Bainbridge's hothouse. Her maid had also carefully threaded seed pearls though her curls.

Her wedding gown was a gift from her grandmother, made from the finest silk and embroidered with a thousand more pearls, fitted to her narrow waist to perfection before falling in soft folds to her feet to make the merest whisper as she moved. After she placed her feet into the matching silk slippers, Helen carefully removed her gold locket and tucked it safely into the sash at her waist. She had nothing of her mother's, but the locket now contained a small blue ribbon, the same shade she remembered her mother loving. She knew she was being fanciful, but she felt that having the locket with her meant, in some way, that her father and mother were there with her.

Finally, her grandmother helped her to fasten the fabulous set of pearls James had sent the day before with a note that read, "These pearls take the place of the bride's tears, so according to custom, you do not have to shed more. I intend to do all I can to ensure that it is so."

Standing beside him in all her finery, with the nobility and the gentry of England sitting silently behind her to witness her marriage, Helen felt as if she were in a dream. She never could have believed that she would one day change from Miss Nobody to Lady Tremaine, Marchioness of Woodville.

James saw Helen glance quickly about the church. He was sure he knew what was on her mind. Their many noble guests, who had been so dismissive of Helen when she had been merely the poor relation, were there. Now that they had seen beyond the lies and half-truths spread by her aunt, they had taken her to their hearts. They had begun to see what he saw—a woman with not only beauty but brains and wit as well. Watching her bloom in society over the last weeks had been one of the greatest pleasures of his life.

James repeated his vows, aware that he did indeed mean every word. He loved Helen with every breath in his body, of course he would cherish her. The thought of her being sick terrified him, but he would remain by her side whatever happened. They had overcome so much already, he was confident that they could face the Devil himself and win if they had to. When the vicar finally announced, "I now pronounce you to be man and wife," James released the breath he had been unaware he had been holding.

The wedding breakfast was held at the Duke of Bainbridge's London mansion. Neither he nor Helen had particularly wanted this large wedding, but the combined wills of the duke and the dowager were not to be denied. A lavish feast had been prepared and a hundred or so had been invited. "I do not know how they managed to arrange all this in so short a time," Helen murmured as yet another course made way to the next.

"The duke told me he had a lifetime of favours to call in and reminded me that he has lived a very long life."

"I wonder if Grandmama did the same."

James chuckled. "According to the duke, he pulled in the favours. Your grandmother merely told people what had to be done and when and they jumped to it."

Helen joined in his laughter. "That does rather sound like Grandmama," she agreed.

After the speeches, Helen whispered, "It is time for me to change, though I really do not want to take off this gown. It makes me feel like a fairy princess."

James' eyes gleamed. "Then do not take it off."

"But I have another for my travelling costume," she replied.

"Do not take it off," he repeated. "Just put a cloak over it. I have a desire to take it off myself to reveal the fairy princess I just married."

"Will it not cause gossip?"

"I imagine it will."

"Do you not care?"

"Not a whit. If people's lives are so dull that they gossip about us, then I consider it our duty to provide them with some diversion in their lives."

"James, you are quite incorrigible."

"I know," he said and grinned.

It was well past sundown by the time they entered James' townhouse, and Helen was reminded of her earlier visit. "Do you mind?" she asked. "That we did not wait for tonight?"

James took both her hands in his. "Of course not," he reassured her. "That night is always in my heart, but tonight is different, because tonight is the first night for us as man and wife, where we can explore and devote ourselves to each other, knowing that we have eternity together. Now, come with me."

The bedroom was as she remembered it. Candles were lit, and a small fire blazed in the grate. She went to unlace her gown, but James' hand stopped her. "No, fairy princess, your husband will serve you in this way." He stood behind her and slowly unlaced her gown, kissing her back as each inch was revealed as Helen watched, fascinated, through the long mirror. Finally, after a tantalizingly long time, her gown was a pool of white at her feet. James held her hand as she stepped out of it.

"Now for the stays," he murmured, turning her again to face the mirror. Once more, he was agonizingly slow as the laces were released. His breath hissed when he saw the lace-trimmed silk chemise and garters holding up her stockings. The silk was so sheer, Helen knew he could see the tightened buds of her nipples.

"Well, fairy princess, what have we here?" he whispered, easing the lacy strap from her shoulders, following them with his warm lips. The garment was quickly dispensed with and for a moment he stood behind her, looking at her reflection in the mirror wearing only her stocking and the pearls he had gifted her, before turning her to face him. She raised her hands to unfasten the necklace. "Leave it on," he said hoarsely. "I once told you I would have you in my bed wearing only jewels. Tonight is the first, but not the last time I intend to do just that, princess."

"I am not a fairy princess, James. I am a real flesh and blood woman, *your* woman," she whispered, her husky voice arousing him further than he thought possible.

"Wife," he corrected.

"Wife," she repeated. "A wife who wants her husband. Now."

His eyes glittered. "Soon, sweetheart, you shall have all of me. Soon." He took her hand and led her to the bed. As she sat, he knelt at her feet and slipped off her wedding slippers, then undid first one garter, then the other, before slowly rolling down her stockings, his fingers caressing her as every inch of flesh was revealed.

Helen was whimpering in sweet agony and he had hardly touched her. "How can you be so controlled, James?" She gasped.

He smiled. "Knowing you, my love, has forced me to be controlled. Tonight though, I want you to be uncontrolled. Other men may see you at the opera, they may even dance with you at balls, but only I will see this part of you, Helen. Only I will truly know you." He gently pushed her knees apart and sought her most intimate place, his tongue delving in and out, paying special and lavish attention to the little bud he knew would give her pleasure.

Helen gripped the edges of the quilt as he relentlessly pleasured her until finally she could hold back no longer, as wave after wave of exquisite pleasure jolted through her body. For a moment it seemed as though the earth had stopped, and without realizing, she cried out his name. He finally raised his head. "That's it, my darling. I want to hear you call my name."

"Oh, James," she whimpered breathlessly. "That was..."

"Pleasant?" he supplied, reminding her of her long-ago description of his kisses.

"Very pleasant," she replied with a gleam in her eye, eagerly awaiting what was to come.

"I'll be damned if my lovemaking is only pleasant," he muttered in mock indignation, quickly divesting himself of his clothing and joining her on the bed. "That," he said, "was merely the hors d'oeuvres, now for the main course."

He rolled her onto her back and trapped her hands above her head with one of his own.

"Is this pleasant?" he asked, rubbing one already sensitized nipple between his thumb and forefinger while sucking and laving the other.

"Or this?" he added, trailing his fingers down her stomach to the curls covering her womanhood.

"Or this? Is this pleasant?" he whispered, his fingers toying with her moist folds before plunging in again and again.

"Oh, James." Helen could scarcely breathe. "Oh, I want..."

"What? What do you want, Helen?" he asked, his voice thick with desire.

"I want you...inside me." She gasped, looking into his eyes. "I want you inside me so that we go there together."

James groaned as he plunged fully into her. His eyes never left hers as he began to move, slowly at first, then, as she began to writhe desperately and move with him, he quickened and deepened his thrusts. He managed to hold on until he felt her clench around him and she once again screamed his name before, with a final thrust, he found his own release.

Panting, he gathered her in his arms. "I take it that was pleasant?" he asked with a smile once he could catch his breath.

"It was incredible," was her muffled response.

"I cannot believe you are finally my wife," he murmured, kissing her hair as they watched the dawn break.

"Whatever brought us together certainly made us wait for our happiness, though it seems to be well worth it," Helen replied. "Now, we had the hors d'oeuvres and the main course. What is for dessert?" she asked as innocently as she could.

"You," he replied, reaching for her again.

EPILOGUE

Two Years Later

*H*er Grace, Helen, Duchess of Bainbridge, looked out of the window of Bainbridge Castle. Despite the size, it managed to feel homey and comfortable as most of the castle was incorporated into the large mansion the previous duke had built. She smiled at the young marquess sleeping peacefully in his bassinet. So much had changed in two years. She was not only accepted by society, she was now considered to be one of the leaders of fashion. If the Duchess of Bainbridge wore a gown, everyone wanted to know where she had purchased it. When she appeared with a new hairstyle, others immediately demanded their maids copy it. It seemed a long time ago that she was Miss Nobody.

Not long after their wedding, there had been great changes in both families. James' sister-in-law, Emily, had given birth to her first child, and of course her own grandmother had been beyond excited to discover she had a grandson. She was never happier than when Johnny took her riding in the park whenever he was down from Eton. For his part, Johnny adored the old lady and enjoyed listening to her stories of his father's escapades as a boy. They would both shortly be coming to the castle to join them for Christmas, as would James' brother, Robert, Emily, their son Stephen, and their new, adorable twins, Eleanor and Rose. The two families took turns to host the holiday house party which seemed to get bigger each year.

Helen frowned. James was late, the light was fading, and the snow which had threatened all day was beginning to fall in large flakes. She was relieved when she saw the light from the two coach lamps in the distance. As soon as he came through the door, he discarded his thick coat and hat and he drew her into his arms for a long, drugging kiss. "I have been thinking about that ever since I left London." He smiled down at her, then stooped over the bassinet to look at his son. "I swear he's grown since I last saw him."

Helen laughed. "You have only been away for two days, Your Grace."

"Two days too long, Your Grace," he growled, kissing her again.

They stood for a few moments by the light of the fire. "I think he would have been proud," James said, indicating the new portrait of the old duke hanging over the fireplace.

"At least he lived to see us married and died knowing there was to be an heir," Helen added.

"And now it is my turn to be proud." He smiled, drawing a copy of *The Times* from his pocket. "'Rarely do novels contain an insight into the human condition with as much clarity and elegance as *Castles in the Air*. I urge readers to buy it and read it, again and again,'" he read.

"Does it really say that?" Helen asked, her eyes shining.

"Oh, there is more, but as to you remaining anonymous, I very much doubt it. 'Those who enjoyed this author's previous work, *The Life of a Moth*, may be interested to know that the writer is, in fact, a lady and a recently ennobled duchess to boot. We await her next work with excited anticipation.' I called to see your Mr. Thompson and he is in raptures, to say the least. I believe you will keep him in good brandy for the rest of his life."

Helen paled and bit her lip. "Oh, dear. That might take longer than I expected."

His face instantly became concerned "What is it, Helen, are you ill?"

"No, not ill, it is just that my energies will be dedicated to something else for the next nine months or so."

James could not hide his joy. "Are you, truly?" he exclaimed.

Helen nodded.

James closed his eyes and raised his head.

After a moment she asked. "What are you doing?"

"Thanking God for the day I met Miss Nobody," he replied, taking her in his arms where she belonged.

THE END

Don't miss out on your next favorite book!

Join the Satin Romance mailing list
www.satinromance.com/mail.html

THANK YOU FOR READING

Did you enjoy this book?

We invite you to leave a review at your favorite book site, such as Goodreads, Amazon, Barnes & Noble, etc.

DID YOU KNOW THAT LEAVING A REVIEW...

- Helps other readers find books they may enjoy.
- Gives you a chance to let your voice be heard.
- Gives authors recognition for their hard work.
- Doesn't have to be long. A sentence or two about why you liked the book will do.

ABOUT THE AUTHOR

Anna lives in a lovely village in Hampshire England with her own romantic hero, otherwise known as her long-suffering husband and has two grown up children. An ex-teacher, she has taught many subjects from religion to drama but has always had a passion for history and would love a time machine to experience life in Georgian England, though suspects she would have been one of the maids washing the cups rather than delicately sipping tea from them.

When she's not thinking about life in the nineteenth century, she enjoys travelling and learning about different customs and cultures, especially the food. Anna also loves to walk in the beautiful Yorkshire Dales which provides much inspiration for her writing. She also plays the piano and it's her ambition to be able to play well enough so that the cat doesn't leave the room.

ALSO BY ANNA AYSGARTH

Unsuitable Brides

A Bride for Christmas

The Marquess Meets Miss Nobody

www.ingramcontent.com/pod-product-compliance
Lightning Source LLC
Chambersburg PA
CBHW020438180626
46812CB00003B/1296